UNCHARTED
The Land Uncharted
Uncharted Redemption
Uncharted Inheritance
Christmas with the Colburns
Uncharted Hope
Uncharted Journey
Uncharted Destiny
Uncharted Promises
Uncharted Freedom
Uncharted Courage
Uncharted Christmas
Uncharted Grace

UNCHARTED BEGINNINGS
Aboard Providence
Above Rubies
All Things Beautiful

ALL THINGS
BEAUTIFUL

KEELY BROOKE KEITH

Edenbrooke
Press

ISBN-13: 9781984039231
ISBN-10: 1984039237

"He has made everything beautiful in its time."
Ecclesiastes 3:11

CHAPTER ONE

The settlement of Good Springs
Late spring, 1868

Hannah Vestal scribbled a story idea on a quartered piece of gray leaf paper. She slipped it back into her apron pocket before anyone could notice. The morning sunlight had yet to peek between the kitchen curtains, and already four of her five hungry siblings were hovering around the table. As she flipped the johnnycakes, the kettle whistled. She poured the steaming water into a copper teapot.

What would Prince Aric think if the maiden Adeline's days began in such a tizzy of feeding family members and packing school lunches?

Hannah checked the underside of the johnnycakes. The batter sizzled on the iron skillet, filling the kitchen with a sweet aroma that reminded her of her mother. While the johnnycakes cooked, she squeezed between the girls to carry the butter dish and the apple jam to the table.

Prince Aric might consider it noble if Adeline had set aside her dreams to help her father raise her younger siblings.

The edges of the cakes turned golden brown. Hannah gripped the skillet's handle with a folded tea towel and dropped the stove cover back into place. Metal clanked sharply against metal, ringing through the farmhouse kitchen, but no one noticed.

Then again, maybe the prince wouldn't appreciate common work no matter the maiden's motivation.

It was a good thing Hannah wasn't writing herself into Adeline's character. The story had changed many times since she'd started writing it during her mother's illness, but over the years since, she'd been careful not to give Adeline her own circumstances. The prince wouldn't be interested in a grown woman who entertained herself by dreaming up stories. What man would?

Hannah passed a milk pitcher to her thirteen-year-old sister. Doris was mid-sentence but didn't miss a syllable as she accepted the pitcher and twirled to the table. "And then Roseanna said that Sarah doesn't like Benjamin anymore since Anthony wrote her a love letter with a poem." Doris held still long enough to hum a wistful sigh. "I hope someday a boy writes me a poem."

Hannah checked a bowl of boiled eggs, which were cooling on an open shelf. "I wish you would stop worrying about boys and focus on your schoolwork."

Breakfast was ready. Looking out the back window, Hannah scanned the property for the rest of her family. Her father and brother were walking toward the house from the orchard. "Here they come."

"Good. I'm starving." Doris rolled one of her two braids between her fingertips. "Hannah, have you seen my pink ribbons anywhere?"

"They are in your second drawer."

Doris snapped her fingers. "I'll be right back."

"No, wait until after we eat." Hannah poured several cups of fresh milk while the seven-year-old twins set the table. The girls' bouncy blond ringlets reminded Hannah of the hair color she'd given Adeline in her story. Surrounded by light-haired girls, it was no wonder she'd written her heroine with the same appearance. But perhaps auburn would suit her character better.

Doris pouted. "But Sarah said we should both wear our pink ribbons today."

One twin bumped the table and milk sloshed out of a cup. Hannah yanked a tea towel from the dish rack and wiped the spill. She glanced at Doris. "It's best to focus on one task at a time. The ribbons can wait."

One of the little girls reached for a boiled egg, but the other protested. "Hannah, she is taking an egg."

Doris swatted the air. "Don't touch the food until after Father says grace."

Hannah gave the girls a motherly glower then forked the johnnycakes onto a platter. "Doris is right," she said to one twin. Then she looked at the other. "And don't snitch on your sister."

"I'm sorry," the twins said in unison. Missing baby teeth added a slur to their apology. Both girls needed their hair combed before school.

The younger of Hannah's two brothers trudged past the stove. She passed the platter to him. "Set this on the table. And don't forget your History report today. Olivia won't let you graduate if you don't turn in your assignments on time."

He groaned. "I know, I know."

"If you know I'm right, then don't grumble." Hannah dabbed her sweaty forehead and moved away from the cook stove. "Doris, did you wash the lunch pails when you got home yesterday?"

"Washed and dried." Doris reached for the pails, which were on the top shelf beside the cook stove. "Did I tell you Olivia will help me make the decorations for the spring dance?"

"You did. And please call her Mrs. McIntosh."

"But you call her Olivia."

"Because she is my friend. You must call her Mrs. McIntosh because she is your teacher."

Doris wrinkled her petite nose, bringing out her lingering childishness. "That's the trouble with being thirteen. I'm half grown up and half kid."

Hannah recalled her teen years. Doris was right about being at an awkward age, but every age had some awkwardness to it. When Hannah had first started writing Adeline and Prince Aric's story, she'd been young and awkward and had written Adeline's character to be the same way. Now, she tried to fold what she'd learned in life into Adeline.

Had she succeeded in maturing her character? She would ask Olivia's opinion on the subject the next time she took pages to her for critique. Those rare afternoons of talking with Olivia about the story were Hannah's only escape from the responsibilities of managing a home. It had been too long since their last visit, but she hadn't written anything new in weeks. She reached into her apron pocket for her notepaper.

Christopher Vestal opened the back door and pulled off his muddy boots. "It will be a great day!"

Hannah smiled at her father as she plucked her pencil from behind her ear. "Plenty of bees in the orchard this morning?"

"The blossoms are humming with the music of spring." He hung his field smock on a peg by the door and climbed the two steps from the mudroom into the kitchen. "Where are my morning kisses?"

The twins scurried to him, giggling. He scooped them up, one in each arm. Their legs dangled as they gave him loud kisses on his clean-shaven cheek. When he'd set the girls down, Doris wrapped her arms around his neck and hugged him as if she were still little. He kissed the top of her head. "Good morning, Kitten."

Hannah studied Doris for a moment. With a long neck and cinched waist, Doris looked more like a young woman than a little girl. How had her little sister grown up so quickly?

Christopher's heels thumped the wooden floor as he walked to his seat at the head of the table. He gave her youngest brother's shoulder a squeeze as he passed. "Did you finish that English paper?"

"History paper," the young man corrected without making eye contact. He scowled at his milk cup.

David ascended the mudroom steps with his dog behind him. He washed his hands in the basin then shoved past Hannah like he owned the place. As the eldest son, this farm would one day be his, but that day was a long time coming. The dog scampered around him, trying to get to the table.

Hannah flicked a wrist at the yellow retriever. "Keep him out of here, please. I scrubbed the floors yesterday, and I'd like it to last more than a day this time."

David smirked. "Give Gideon some respect. He became a proud papa of eight last night."

Doris shot up so quickly her chair squeaked. "The puppies were born?"

The twins ran to the door. "Can we see them? Can we?"

"After breakfast," their father answered, his voice stern but kind. "Come sit down, girls."

Hannah carried a pewter plate of sliced cheese to the table and placed it near her father. She sat next to David and glanced at the empty chair at the end of the long table. She meant to look for only a second, to acknowledge her late mother as she did at every meal, but while her father said the blessing, Hannah's eyes never closed.

A layer of dust dulled the ladder-back slats of the dining chair. She should have kept it cleaner. She had meant to. Doris did the dusting last week. Hannah would do it herself this week. That's what she had promised her mother—not the dusting specifically, but to take care of everything: the home and her siblings, to raise them, to protect them, to teach the girls to be women who would one day take care of their own households.

She had promised to put her family first. Her father, David, Wade, Doris, Ida, and Minnie—they all depended on her to keep that promise. *Put them before your friends and your schooling,* Mother had said. *Keep writing your stories, but put your family first. They need you.*

Five and a half years later, they still needed her. She touched the folded-up paper in her apron pocket. They needed her and she needed to write. Creating her story made it easier to stay dedicated to her promise and not yearn for a life apart from this house.

The imaginative process wasn't enough though. It was the actual pencil to page that made the story come alive. If only she had more time—time alone, time to write, time to think. The busyness of a full house kept her on her feet and at the stove for hours each day, and school would be out soon, so there would be even more voices and more needs to put before her own.

She had promised to raise her siblings, but the twins were only seven now. Could she do this for a decade more? The weight of the years pushed on her shoulders as if she were strapped with a fifty-pound sack of flour. How pleasant it would feel to drop that sack and run! But no. These people were her family, the anchor of her promise.

Still, the glum ache remained. She could only write that yearning, that desperate stirring for something more, into Adeline's story.

As Christopher said *Amen*, Hannah closed her eyes and opened them again, this time careful not to look at her mother's dusty chair. The twins needed help with peeling eggs, and Doris's chatter rose over the twins' whining about seeing the puppies.

Her brothers held a quieter conversation about the dogs and which family in the village would get one. Christopher interrupted them. "We must offer the puppies to those in village-supported positions before trading with other families. I doubt the reverend, the doctor, or our schoolteacher will want another dog, but we must ask them first. Then we'll talk about the puppies that are left." He looked past the twins and winked at Hannah. "Delicious breakfast."

Her father's approval made everything feel better. Almost everything.

After they ate, she packed the children's lunches while Doris dashed into the bedroom she and Hannah shared. Doris plodded out a moment later, frowning. A pink ribbon dangled from the end of one of her braids. She touched the other braid. "I guess I've lost one of my ribbons somewhere. I don't remember when I wore them last."

Hannah covered each lunch pail with a square of cheesecloth and tied it with twine. "Forget about the ribbon and come get your lunch pail."

"I can't go to school today." Doris's chin quivered. "I can't be seen like this."

Hannah's father and David were already back to work in the orchard, and the other children were standing on the stoop, waiting to walk to school with Doris. There was always some stall, some lost item, some emotional upheaval before school, but once she got the children out the door, the day was hers to do her housework and to think.

Hannah wiped her hands on her apron and turned Doris around. She untied the long pink ribbon and draped it over her sister's shoulder as she unwound the two braids. Using the same gentle touch her mother had used with her, she combed out Doris's dishwater blond waves and wove them into one thick plait. The kitchen fell quiet, save for Doris's sniffles.

"I remember the way it feels," Hannah said. She tied the ribbon into the prettiest bow possible. "Wanting the other girls to like you, wanting to feel pretty. You are as pretty as Sarah Ashton and Roseanna Colburn and the others."

Doris turned, pulling the fresh braid to the front of her dress. The tip of her nose was as pink as the ribbon. "But all the boys like Sarah."

"Things change very quickly at your age. They might all like her today and all like you tomorrow."

"Did that ever happen to you?"

Hannah had spent her early teen years helping her bedridden mother with twin infants while her father planted the orchard. There hadn't been time for school or ribbons or boys. The isolation had stopped bothering her once she started writing, but looking back, a lonely pang echoed inside her heart. She rubbed Doris's arm. "My adolescence differed greatly from yours. Enjoy your freedom and your friends."

Doris pointed at the ribbon. "Thank you."

"You're welcome."

"You sound like her... like Mother. Sometimes I dream about her and hear her voice. When I awaken, I realize it was your voice in my dream." Doris spun to pick up her schoolbooks from the edge of the table, leaving Hannah gaping as the words took hold. Her sister had spent as many years being cared for by her as by their mother. Doris's young mind had given their mother's image Hannah's voice.

The significance of Hannah's influence on the children pressed her insides together. Her siblings had no mother, but they had her and would as long as they needed her. She passed a lunch pail to each of the girls and a second pail to Doris. "Hand this to Wade, please."

She closed the door and waved goodbye through the window in the back door. Her breath fogged the glass, which had once been a window in the sterncastle of the ship that brought them to this uncharted land. After that arduous voyage aboard the *Providence*, the families had spent years building the settlement of Good Springs, but before she could enjoy the new village and schoolhouse, her mother passed away, entrusting her with the task of mothering five children.

A stack of dirty dishes called to her as did the dough that needed baking and laundry that needed washing. She traced a finger over the folded piece of paper in her pocket. She might not have the freedom to choose her lot or experience her own romance, but she was the master of her stories, the creator and controller of an ideal universe where adventure awaited, health abounded, and love made people glad to be alive.

If she couldn't have the life she dreamed of, she could create it for Adeline and Aric. They deserved to live happily ever after. Now if only she could finish her story in a way she felt was worthy of her noble characters, even though no one besides Olivia would ever read it.

CHAPTER TWO

Henry Roberts loathed waiting for his brother. He worked better at the letterpress by himself anyway. If Simon hoped to improve his typesetting skills, he should have come straight to the print shop after breakfast too.

Henry rubbed the palm of his left hand and stretched it wide, trying to relieve the phantom itching in his two missing fingers. Keeping himself busy at the press helped to keep his mind off it. His hands were as eager to set type as he was. Only a few more pages to print for an order of eight readers for the school and he could work on his next project: *Shakespeare's Sonnets*. He checked his pocket watch. It was pointless to wait for Simon any longer.

Henry stepped to the shop door and picked through a box of sorts, examining the copper-platted letters in the early morning light. After years of learning what had been his father's trade back in Virginia, Henry's letterpress skills now surpassed his father's. Though his brother had learned the trade too, Simon's pages were far inferior, certainly not worth binding.

Reverend William Colburn walked past the print shop. He pushed his spectacles higher on his nose. "Good morning, Henry."

Henry tucked his half-hand into his apron pocket. "Good morning, Reverend." He nodded politely then returned to the worktable inside. He found the letters he needed for the final pages and set the sorts in the bed of the press, carefully aligning the type. Precision in the row produced excellence on the page. Every page deserved perfection.

The late spring wind blew loose petals past the doorway. Henry glanced up, expecting to see Simon. A stack of yesterday's misprints rustled beneath a rock on the desk. If Simon came to the print shop today, Henry would have him find the sorts instead of setting type. A helper might speed the work, but he wasn't in the mood to waste ink and paper on Simon's shoddy work today.

Nor was he in the mood to teach.

Teaching slowed him. Henry's father had taught him well and had known when to let go. That's when Henry's enjoyment of the letterpress grew into passion. If he did nothing else for the rest of his life but print and bind books, he would die a satisfied man.

A satisfied man with a disfigured hand.

Of course, he would spend his life making improvements to the press. There was no such thing as a perfect process. If that fact wasn't obvious in making books, it was obvious in the way Good Springs was being governed. Only one elder from each of the eight families that formed the settlement had a voice in the weekly council meetings. As the oldest son who would one day inherit his father's position on the council, Henry had spent years attending those meetings in silence.

The elder council expected the next generation to learn by listening, but the leaders had too much control. Ideas for improvements had swirled inside Henry's mind, locked behind closed lips during the weekly meetings. A man could only tolerate mediocrity for so long. The flawed system needed an overhaul.

He squatted to open one of the thin drawers at the bottom of the press cabinet. An array of rarely used sorts crowded the drawer. The way his father organized the type needed an overhaul as well. If Henry was going to continue to share the print shop with his father, they needed to have a talk about organization.

A man's voice carried on the wind, and a moment later a shadow darkened the shop. Henry continued setting type and didn't look away from the rows of reversed letters. "You're late again, Simon."

"With good reason." Simon stepped into the print shop but stayed in the doorway, leaving on his straw hat. His bottom lip protruded the way it had since they were children, making him look unhappy even when he wasn't.

Their father walked in too, but he was grinning wide enough to puff his gray side whiskers. "We had a calf born this morning, Henry. You should see her. Beautiful cow. That's three so far this spring."

"I'm glad you're pleased." Henry continued working. "Will you have the paper finished in time for me to start my next project this afternoon?"

"I should, yes." Matthew Roberts scratched his cheek as he moved to the type cabinet. He opened one of the drawers Henry had reorganized. "You run your print shop far more efficiently than I ever ran mine and produce much finer pages than I did."

Henry dislodged his attention from the letterpress. "This is your shop, Father."

Matthew closed the drawer and studied Henry, his eyes sharply focused beneath his drooping brow. "It's time we made some changes, son."

Simon smirked and his thick bottom lip curved.

Henry wiped his fingertips on a dry rag and stuffed it into his back pocket. "What kind of changes?"

Matthew lifted his chin toward the letterpress. "I brought all this from Virginia to teach you my trade. You mastered it. Now that I've developed an efficient method of making paper from the gray leaf tree pulp, I want to give that my full attention. And your brother," he motioned toward Simon, "isn't suited for indoor work. He has taken to the farming."

Henry crossed his arms. "What are you saying?"

Matthew rested his palms on the edge of the worktable and leaned forward. His mouth worked, adjusting his porcelain false teeth. "It's my duty as a founder of this settlement to make sure my sons have work that sustains them and improves the settlement. You are the firstborn, and I intended for you to take over the farm, but things aren't going the way I planned when we first settled here."

Henry looked out the window at the new stone building next door. The empty library's tapered door—made from the planks of the *Providence*—stood ajar. He'd much rather print the books needed to fill the settlement's library than work on the farm, especially after the accident. He rubbed the scarred nubs where his pinkie and ring finger had been torn off. "Are you dissatisfied with my preference for print work?"

"No, son, I'm not. You followed my footsteps, and now I've found something that demands my attention more than printing. The elders agree with me that I should focus my time on making paper for the village. I'll still care for our livestock, but Simon will manage the fields. I want you to take over the print shop… permanently. It's time for you to have your own livelihood."

"Livelihood?" Henry's gaze dropped to the rows of letters awaiting ink. He loved the work and planned to move away from home someday, but running the press all day wouldn't leave time to clear land and build a house and plant and harvest food. He needed his father's involvement in the print work to justify his still living at home. "I've had a few orders, but there isn't enough work for me to trade for a living. I'm not charging anyone for this order of books for the school." He picked up a jar of freshly mixed ink and stirred it. The air filled with the mixture of soot and walnut oil. He breathed in the aroma. "I wish this were a living, but it isn't. Not yet. I would have to spend my time planting and hunting just to survive."

Matthew looked at Henry's damaged hand and compassion filled his voice. "You have a bed at my home—always will, unless you marry."

Simon snickered. At first it rankled, but then Henry joined him. It was true: he would never marry. No woman wanted a man with half a hand, and he didn't know a woman in the village who would warrant the effort of courting. Women required too much adoration and still found offense at a man's every comment and gesture.

Matthew examined a page hanging up to dry. "Son, with your skill and speed at the press, I believe you could produce enough books for the library and school and church to earn a living."

"You talk as though the elders would make the press a village-supported trade. Last I heard they planned to fill the library over the centuries. Did I miss something in one of the meetings?"

His father brushed Simon's shoulder. "Go on back to the farm. I'll be there shortly."

After Simon left, Matthew walked to the doorway. He pointed toward the stone building next door. "The elders wouldn't have approved the building of a library if books weren't important to this village."

Henry recalled the elders' meetings before the library was built—the mulling of petitions, the allocating of resources, and the hours of deliberation on the books that might one day fill it. It had taken all of his strength to not jump into the debates on either side; it wouldn't have mattered which side so long as his voice had been heard. Between the meetings, he'd had his father's ear. That was when he'd been able to influence the progress. "They approved the library because you were the printer and would be in charge of creating and maintaining the collection."

"Son, I'm no librarian."

"Nor am I."

"I'm a papermaker."

"And you already support your family with the farm."

Matthew lifted an authoritative brow. "The print shop should be your occupation. We will get you the orders you need to trade for a living. I could help you with the press at first, but you don't need me."

"I work better by myself." Henry scanned the one-room former cabin. From the impeccably arranged top drawers of type to the organized worktable, every detail of the print shop was falling under his management. His father had already given him control, and it was time he accepted it. "The village needs paper and you could produce enough if Simon took over the farming. The village also needs a printer and should support the making of books."

"Then we agree." Matthew rubbed his wooly side whiskers. "I will speak to the elders."

Agreeing with his father didn't mean he would get his way with the elder council. He shook his head. "Since this involves me, I prefer to speak for myself."

"As the elder, I must present the requests from my family to the council. They will have questions for you, to be sure, but I see no reason for them to deny you the living."

In the eight years since the families of Good Springs gathered at the Ashton family's estate in Accomack County and planned the group migration, the one thing Henry had come to expect was a fervent debate on every issue. This time their debate would determine his future. The challenge lit a spark in his chest. "And if the elders object, there is always room for persuasion."

"Persuasion?" Matthew chuckled as he walked out. "If you could make a living out of that, you would be the richest man in the Land."

CHAPTER THREE

Hannah flipped through a stack of loose pages until she found the scene in her story she wanted to revise. In the soft light of her oil lamp, her tired eyes lost focus, blurring the pencil markings. She leaned over her narrow writing desk and mindlessly tapped her fingers on the page in dull thumps. Her scene needed a complete rewrite.

Doris stirred in her sleep, rustling the quilt on her side of the bed they shared. Hannah's fingers stilled their tapping. She should go to bed, but her characters wouldn't let her rest. With the children asleep, she could finally hear her own thoughts, which were filled with snippets of a story she'd tried to tell for years.

The story barely resembled her first naive draft. Originally, the young maiden Adeline's epic adventure began when she was forced to take a perilous voyage across a monster-filled sea. The sentences were strings of flowery prose Hannah's mind had compiled from old fairy tale books.

She'd read those first chapters to her pregnant mother, who always summoned the strength to smile and praise her talent. After the twins were born, her mother's illness worsened. Hannah's days were long and draining, but her desperate imagination raced with creative energy. She poured her soul onto the page by adding a love story to the adventurous plot. Adeline survived the voyage to a foreign land and met Aric, the brave and prosperous prince.

When Hannah's mother passed away, the story felt simplistic, worthless. Without her mother's approval and input, she questioned everything she wrote. She summoned the courage to ask Olivia to read it in secret. Olivia made grammar and spelling corrections, but it was her advice on plot and character that ignited Hannah's desire to reshape the story into a masterpiece, though no one else would ever read it.

Suspenseful layers began to develop. Adeline and Aric were forbidden to court, so they had to meet secretly to evade the evil queen. Just when they had formed a plan to marry, Adeline was captured by a neighboring kingdom and forced into slavery.

Olivia had lauded the way Hannah changed the story and encouraged her to keep growing in her craft.

Now Adeline's character yearned to stretch beyond her storybook limitations. She wasn't happy with the future Prince Aric offered. Ambition was bubbling inside her, but she had no goal to challenge her and prove her strength. Maybe there was something bigger for Adeline back in her homeland. Maybe not. Either way, she couldn't spend her life sitting prettily in a musty castle while the prince was away on his own adventures.

Doris stirred again, and Hannah feared she was unsettling her sister by keeping the light burning so late. She tucked her last piece of blank paper under her elbow, slid a pencil behind her ear, and carried her lamp through the parlor, walking carefully, quietly.

As she rounded the fireplace and stepped into the kitchen, the glow from her lamp illumined a figure at the far end of the table. Her pulse quickened before recognition set in. "Father? What are you doing up?"

Christopher raked his fingers through his loose, gray hair. "Couldn't sleep. You?"

"I could sleep if I went to bed, but I need to write." She set her lamp on the center of the table. "Would you like a cup of water?"

He shook his head and grinned a little, but it didn't reach his eyes. "You used to say *want*."

"Hm?"

"You used to say you *want* to write. Now you say you *need* to write."

She filled a cup halfway then sat in front of her lamp, leaving two empty chairs between her and her father. "I don't think it means anything."

"I do." Christopher propped his elbows on the table and peered at her over his folded hands. Fatigue softened his kind eyes. "What are you writing about tonight?"

"I don't know."

"Or you want to keep it to yourself?"

"No, I really don't know where to start." She broke his gaze. "And yes, I prefer to keep my writing to myself."

He leaned back in his chair and tucked one hand into his nightshirt. He used to only do that when the room was cold, but as he got older, he did it more often. "Your mother loved hearing your story."

He let the silence hang as if his statement were a question.

Hannah had no reason to keep her writing from her father, nor did she have a reason to believe he would appreciate it. Oh, he would understand the words and the actions. He'd probably praise her efforts, but the deeper nuances of Adeline's yearning and Aric's appeal would be lost on him. It would be lost on anyone, except her mother and Olivia.

When she didn't reply, he tried again, tapping a finger on her blank page this time. "And I'm sure it's a good story or Olivia wouldn't keep helping you with it after all these years."

"She's taught me grammar and the finer points of storytelling that she says all the great writers must learn."

"God has bestowed upon you a zeal for your craft in addition to natural talent. I hope you will share your writing with me someday." His voice lessened in volume, bearing the sadness of loss. "Your mother wanted you to finish the story."

Hannah's gaze shot to him. "I did. I have finished it. Many times." She thought of all the changes she'd made over the years and stared at the blank paper. "But then I'm not satisfied with it, and I go back and change the story. And then I have to rewrite other parts."

"Perhaps you don't want it to end."

Of course, she wanted her story to end. What would be the point of writing every day if there were no completion? Every day for years, the scenes had played in her mind as she'd cooked and cleaned and bathed muddy children. She'd physically worked to keep her promise to her mother, and she'd mentally worked on her story to finish it. "Completion is eluding me, that's all."

"What do you need?"

She flipped up the corner of her last blank page. "More paper."

"I'll find something to take to Mr. Roberts tomorrow and trade for paper."

"No, I want to trade for my own paper. I'll take him some of the extra candles I made."

"Very well." Her father tilted his head. "However, I suspect you need more than paper."

She shrugged, awaiting his suggestion.

"Perhaps you need the motivation to finish the story."

"I have a motivator… satisfaction. I want to finish the story in a way that pleases me."

"By when?"

She shrugged again.

"For whom?"

She didn't understand his question. "For me." When he gazed blankly, she tried once more. "For Mother?"

He remained silent for a moment, staring at his hands then he shifted in his seat. "My father, your Grandpa Vestal, died a week after his fiftieth birthday. I didn't receive word until a month after his passing. The news of his death came as a shock. He'd been a robust man, no sign of illness. His heart gave out at only fifty years of age."

Hannah listened, half wishing she could sit in the lamplight with her father all night and half wishing he'd go to bed so she could be alone and write.

"I think of his death more often now that my fiftieth birthday is approaching."

"Your birthday is in March. Today is the Sixteenth of November."

He held up a finger. "The Seventeenth. It's past midnight."

"Still, your birthday is four months away."

"Four months spends quickly at my age, dear." He grinned, creasing the skin around his eyes, but solemnness replaced his pleasant expression. "Life spends quickly at my age… at any age. I hope you will share your story while I'm still around to read it."

His suggestion bore a hole in her heart. She touched his hand and rubbed his rough knuckles. "You can't believe your life might end at fifty because your father's did. Would you want me to believe my life will end at thirty-four because Mother's did? I'm past twenty now, so that doesn't leave me much time."

"No, no, sweet girl." He patted her arm. "I only meant that life is brief. You are wonderful with the children. I can't imagine what I would have done these past few years without you. Your mother always said you were a natural storyteller and a gifted writer. As a father, I want to see you use your God-given talents. And I hope to see it in my lifetime, however long or short that might be."

Though his words were meant to encourage, the sting of guilt was rising in her throat. "I am using my talent. I write every day."

He lifted a hand, halting her defense. "You are hiding your light under a bushel. If God gave you a message to share through story, share it."

"I feel ill even thinking of others reading my work."

He pressed his lips together and nodded once as if he understood more about her than she did. "Graveyards are full of unshared talent. Imagine what a blessing it would be to the people of this village to have a fresh story to read, for the generations to come to have more stories to study, for that one person who needs your words someday. Write the story with the message God gave you. Trust Him with the rest."

He stood and slid his chair beneath the table's edge. As he passed behind her, he kissed the top of her head. "Goodnight, sweet Hannah."

The floorboards creaked softly as he stepped into his bedroom and closed the door. Hannah lowered her hands to her lap. She'd never imagined others being blessed by reading her story, only her being embarrassed—nay, terrified—to think of anyone but Olivia knowing what scenes played out in her imagination.

Wasn't a mind created to be private? Couldn't a writer express herself for the sake of expression and not for exposure?

Despite her objections, her father's words took root. Many times she'd wished for a new book to read, a new story to get lost in after her mother's death—not immediately after but months later when the neighbors had stopped checking in and everyone else's grief had subsided.

She didn't know of any other writers in the village. If she was the only one and God had truly given her a gift that should be shared, she wouldn't want to be guilty of taking her talent to the grave.

But the story wasn't finished, not in its present state. She had a few ideas of where it needed to be changed. Still, something was lacking. Even if she wrote a story that would be a light for someone someday, she needed inspiration and time… and paper.

Her father wanted to read the story in his lifetime and had mentioned his fiftieth birthday. What if she finished the story and gave him a copy on his birthday? No, that would be impossible. The story needed more work than she could do in four months, especially with the way her inspiration had stalled.

Her father was the only person alive who knew about her story but hadn't read it. She hadn't allowed him. Why not? He could be trusted. He wouldn't mock her if he didn't like the story.

If he wanted to read her story, she would grant him permission… more than permission. Somehow, someway, she would finish it in time to give him a copy on his birthday.

"Write the story with the message God gave you," she repeated her father's words on a whisper. "Trust Him with the rest."

CHAPTER FOUR

Henry dropped a wrapped biscuit into his bag then looped the satchel's strap over his shoulder as he left home for the print shop. Bright morning rays pierced between the gray leaf trees on his parents' property. A warm wind blew in from the nearby ocean, filling the late spring air with its salty scent.

He passed beneath the clothesline where his mother was already hanging the laundry. "Goodbye, Mother."

"Will you be home for supper this evening?" Priscilla Roberts asked him. Strands of brown and gray escaped her loose bun of hair and danced in the breeze.

He kept walking but glanced at her over his shoulder. "Yes. Then we have an elders' meeting tonight."

"A very important meeting, I hear." She smiled, warming his heart. "I'm boiling crab for supper. Your favorite."

In twenty-six years, his mother had never failed to prepare her children's choice meal to mark special occasions. If the elders approved his father's request to make printing a village-supported trade, tonight's meeting would not be simply a special occasion, it would be a historic event. The elders had never agreed on a village matter the same night it was presented.

He dodged a row of hanging socks at the end of the clothesline. "I look forward to dinner."

As he walked between the southern side of his family's house and the barn, weeds brushed his trouser cuffs. Simon needed to cut the grass soon, or their father. Regardless, it wouldn't be his chore anymore if he were going to work full time at the press. The thought brought a sense of relief, like when a sore throat finally went away.

Domestic chores squeezed the breath out of a thinking man. If he owned the place, he might feel differently. The village elders took pride in keeping their farms pleasant and productive, as the women did their homes, which explained the sighs and complaints of his sisters when they had come of age; it wasn't their kitchen, so they tired of cleaning it. Just as this wasn't his yard, so he tired of mowing it.

As a contented bachelor with a village-supported occupation, he would never have to worry about such things. His days would be spent printing and binding books; the men in the village would build him a cabin or add living quarters to the print shop. He would select what he needed from the weekly market, barter private orders of books for small luxuries, and go fishing in between.

The status quo of farming and family life would never have a hold on him. He'd never lose another finger raising a barn again.

He ambled along the road into the village, passing house after house that he'd helped build when they settled the area years ago. Since then, Gabe McIntosh and his father had built bigger homes for all the families. Tradesmen like his father had turned old cabins into workshops. Reverend Colburn had established a church, and Olivia Owens—now Olivia McIntosh—had started a school. And all the settlers came together every Saturday morning on the sandy lot next to the school to trade their produce and wares. Soon, he'd have a batch of six leather-bound copies of *Shakespeare's Sonnets*, two for the library and four to trade.

Stepping inside the dark print shop, he propped the door open to receive as much morning sunlight as possible. The scents of ink and copper greeted him. He lowered his satchel to the floor between the press and the far wall then paused by the window.

Next door, the stone library stood cold and empty, begging to be filled with books. It would be his duty if all went well at the elders' meeting tonight.

A light knock on the open door disrupted his quiet. Hannah Vestal, the neighbor girl from the property north of his parents' farm, dithered in the doorway. She held a basket full of candles. "Excuse me, will Mr. Roberts be here soon?"

"My father is working at home today."

"Oh." Her gaze lowered to the candles. "I was hoping to trade these for paper?"

Henry studied her for a moment, struck by the oddity of seeing Hannah Vestal somewhere other than church. The years of seclusion since her mother's death made her a mystery to him. She must be a slave to her siblings' upbringing. Though demure in appearance, something about her high cheekbones and dark lashes veiled innate nobility, shirking the impression of servitude.

The eldest of the Vestal children had grown into an attractive woman. Still, Henry would always see her as the mournful teen weeping over her mother's fresh grave years ago. He had left Mrs. Vestal's funeral and gone home to weep that day too, grieving the loss as everyone in the settlement had. The only way he'd overcome it was by sketching Mrs. Vestal's portrait, not the way she had looked in those final months of life, but the way she looked when the group lived in Virginia. She'd been strong, majestic almost, with the same high cheekbones as the woman standing before him now.

Remembering the pain, his heart stirred with an overwhelming desire to help Hannah in any way he could. He waved his good hand at the rolls of paper beside a cut table at the back of the shop. "I have plenty of paper and happen to need candles."

She didn't immediately respond. Had she not heard him or not understood his reply? He rounded the press and stopped at the worktable. "On cloudy days, it's almost too dark in here to work."

A slow smile graced her rosy lips. "Excellent, or rather, not that your workshop is dim, but I mean it is excellent that you should need candles." Her cheeks flushed, matching her pink lips. "For me, anyway, because I have two dozen here to trade for paper."

He reached into the basket and drew out a pair of tapers, which were still attached at the wick. "That's a lot of candles to trade for paper. I'll take four. Save the rest to trade at the market."

Her smile vanished. She took a half step closer and whispered, "I need quite a lot of paper."

The secretive manner of her voice over something as trivial as trading candles for paper almost made him laugh. He held it back not wanting to mock such a delicate creature. Leaning down to whisper too, he asked, "How much paper?"

"Two hundred sheets."

"You're right. That is quite a lot." He stood straight and grinned at her. "Why are we whispering?"

The light shining through the doorway highlighted the golden flecks in her brown eyes. She leveled her glowing gaze on him, bucking all notion of fragility. "I prefer to keep my business affairs private. If you aren't accustomed to trading discretely, I can trade with your father. He never questions me."

He laced his voice with sarcasm. "Pardon my insensitivity. The secrecy you employ over a trade for paper piqued my curiosity."

The punch of his humor seemed as lost on her as it was on any woman. She bowed her regal neck a degree as if deigning to accept his apology. "No harm done."

Perhaps she was being sarcastic too. If he knew her more, he'd be able to read her intentions or at least be able to provoke her and then read her reaction. Considering her simple life, it seemed more likely she was taking him at his word. A twinge of guilt tightened his chest.

What was it about women that always put him on guard? He gave her unimposing stature a quick study. She was too small to be threatening, so his defensiveness must be unwarranted. He cleared the cynicism from his throat. "I take great care in stocking and cutting my paper and like to be assured it will go to good use." He returned the taper candles to her basket and rested both palms on the worktable. "Why do you need so much paper?"

Her gaze darted around the print shop. "I'd rather…
I'd rather not say."

The noblewoman was gone and the homebody was
back. Had he flustered her by being male or did she need
the paper for a truly private endeavor? Either way, there
was something amusing about pressing her further. "Did
your sisters lose their school slates?"

"No."

"Are you papering your walls?"

She squared her shoulders and hiked the basket up to
her chest. "Will you trade with me or not?"

"You don't have enough candles to trade for two
hundred sheets of paper."

She plunked her basket on the press table, her
assertiveness ignited. "How much paper will you give me
for all of these?"

The force in her voice fueled his urge to vex her for
the pleasure of watching her stir. However, knowing the
woman before him encased a mournful girl who needed
something he had to offer, he decided against jesting and
drew several candles out of the basket.

The smooth candles were solid with tightly woven
wicks, and he needed them. He removed all but four of
the candles, unable to take everything she had. "I will
accept these for twenty sheets of paper."

"But I need two hundred sheets."

She didn't need that much paper. Something was
amiss. He pointed at the tall rolls of paper filling a wide
bin beside the cut table in the back corner of the room.
"Each of those rolls contains only twelve sheets of
paper." When her eyes widened, he asked, "Are you
certain you require two hundred sheets?"

"Oh, no." A burst of laughter broke her regality. She pressed her hand to her middle. "I'm sorry. No wonder you looked confused. I need two hundred pages—as in sheets of writing paper." She drew a rectangle in the air. "About this size."

Delighted by her laughter, his eyes refused to look away as he pulled a paper roll from the bin and opened it on the cut table. Little lines curved around her mouth when she laughed, almost like dimples but more stately.

The smile lines faded along with her laughter, and he wanted to see them again. The yearning pressed him to say something humorous, anything to make her laugh again, but his mind went as blank as the paper he was unrolling. He stood open-jawed as if every ounce of his intelligence had been doused by her song-like laughter.

His half-hand lost what little strength it had, and he fumbled with the paper roll. For a moment time seemed to freeze. Her gaze darted to his scars, and pity changed her expression. He would rather receive disgust than pity. Wanting neither from her, he fought to appear composed. "Yes, well, I will trade you the candles for writing paper... two hundred pages. About six inches by nine then?"

She nodded. "Sounds right. I've never measured. Your father always cut the pages for me."

"We get eight pages of six by nine per sheet." He tried to focus on the paper, though her gaze had yet to leave his hand. "So you only need twenty-five sheets, not two hundred."

She pointed at the door. "Should I come back for it tomorrow?"

"No, unless you're in a rush. It will only take me a few minutes."

"Very well." She folded her hands and glanced about the room. "This was the Fosters' cabin before it was your father's print shop, wasn't it?"

"It was."

"Do you know if Mr. Foster will play his violin at the spring dance this year?"

"I haven't heard." He looked up from the paper to study her form as she ambled to the letterpress. "Will you be at the dance?"

"I'm a chaperone."

"What are you going to write?"

"At the dance?"

"No, on this paper."

She snapped her face toward him. "I beg your pardon?"

"Most people order writing paper a dozen pages at a time. Even the reverend only orders twice that, and he writes a sermon every week." He marked the pages for cutting but kept eyeing her. "Why do you need two hundred pages?"

"I like to stay well stocked."

"This should last you a lifetime."

She mumbled, "I will use it up in four months."

"You must be writing a book."

"Pardon?"

"To use two hundred pages in four months, you must be writing a book. Is it a work of fiction? A love story, perhaps?"

"Never you mind." Her regal chin lifted. She silently inspected the rows of letters he'd set in the press last night. The only sound came from the swish of the cutting blade through the paper.

He wanted to push her for answers, but she turned her face away. Her profile looked as it had at the gravesite all those years ago. This woman was not to be pushed or teased. It was a shame though as something about her stirred a longing in his soul.

CHAPTER FIVE

Hannah eyed the shelf of gray clouds moving in from the ocean as she plucked the clothespins off the dried laundry. The humid air carried the fresh scent of coming rain. The children would be home from school any minute, and she'd yet to create a plot thread reconciling Adeline's desire to return to her homeland and her love for Aric. Her story made little sense.

Hannah stared into her full laundry basket. Why would a woman who had found true love with a brave prince suddenly want to be elsewhere? The answer eluded her.

Why had she thought she could finish the story in four months?

She pulled a piece of folded notepaper out of her pocket and opened it. Crowded words almost too small to read filled the page, yet she had two hundred blank pages in her desk drawer waiting for her to fill them with inspired prose. At this rate, the paper would remain as blank as it was when Henry had cut it this morning.

Two hundred pages not sheets, he'd said.

At least he'd been kind about her blunder. He had looked at her oddly while he cut the pages—almost as though he was embarrassed by something. But then he'd questioned her about what she was writing. Why did he think he had the authority to say how the paper could be used?

Before she could dismiss Henry, she thought of Aric. Perhaps he too would have assertive qualities. He was a prince and had been raised in a privileged lifestyle, so it would make sense if he had strong opinions and forced them on others. Was that assertiveness, though, or simply arrogance? She would have to think about it more to apply it to Prince Aric, but as for Henry Roberts, she couldn't say. She barely knew the man, but he seemed to possess both assertiveness and arrogance in abundance.

Prince Aric needed more complexities added to his personality, and Henry Roberts might provide examples. She glanced toward the Roberts' property. An acre of blooming apple trees stood between her and the woods that separated their families' farms. He lived next door, yet she only saw him in passing at church on Sundays. Did Henry's heart have as many scars as his left hand?

She started to make a note on her page when the barn door slammed shut across the yard. A moment later, David walked past the clothesline and swiped the page from her hand. He scowled at her. "Why are you always scribbling? Shouldn't you be working?"

"Give that back!" she demanded of her brother.

He flipped her notepaper around to read it then stopped and crinkled his brow. "This is gibberish."

She reached for the page, but he moved away too quickly. Every muscle in her body wanted to jump at him and fight to get her private page out of his dirty hands.

She would have fought him when they were children. That was probably the reaction he was hoping for. Though David was two years her junior, he was a foot taller than her and a grown man. She wasn't a child anymore either and hadn't been for a long time.

She returned her attention to the clothesline, pretending not to care that he was looking at her private notes. "Perhaps if you had finished school, you would be able to read my gibberish."

He squinted at the page. "Prince? You don't still write your little fairy tales, do you?"

She hadn't realized he knew anything about her stories. Her cheeks burned. "Mind your own business!"

David held the page out to her, pinching its corner as if it were covered in bird dung. "No wonder you always look tired. Maybe if you put away your childish love stories, you could focus on your housework."

She snatched the paper from him and shoved it into her apron. The sound of a short tear came from her pocket, rousing the ever-present ache of disappointment. "Go away, David. Don't you have work to do?"

"I could ask you the same. You promised Mother you would take care of the house, remember?"

Before she could form a bold retort, Christopher's voice boomed from behind them. "Leave her alone."

She glowered at David until he walked away, then she unpinned the last of the laundry and hefted the basket to the house. "Thank you, Father."

Christopher opened the mudroom door for her. "A storm is coming."

Her four youngest siblings strode toward the orchard from the road, books in their arms and empty lunch pails swinging from their wrists. Hannah grinned at her father. "Are you speaking of the rain clouds or of them?"

He chuckled then gazed at the road and paused abruptly. "Oh. Olivia is with them."

"She is coming to help Doris with the decorations for the spring dance."

"Very well." His eyes scanned the sky as he left the stoop. "The clouds are tall. The rain will pass as quickly as it comes. Give Olivia my best. I need to do some work in the barn."

The back door blew closed behind Hannah. She stood in the mudroom, peering through the window. Her father waved jovially at the children and raised his hat to Olivia as he rushed toward the barn. He always seemed in a hurry to hide himself when Olivia came around.

A chorus of thuds shook the mudroom as the children scuttled onto the stoop. Hannah opened the door for them. "Hello Minnie, Ida," she greeted the twins as they passed. "Wade, shoes off."

Doris dashed past her. "Do we have a spare basket? I'm off to collect flowers, and Mrs. McIntosh is going to show me how to dry them so they will be perfect for the spring dance decorations."

"Hello to you too," Hannah said to Doris's back as her sister raced to their bedroom to look for a basket.

Hannah turned to greet Olivia. The giddy thrill of a friend's presence in her home made her clasp her hands over her heart. "Come in, come in. I'm so glad you're here!"

Olivia stepped inside, beaming. She smoothed back windswept strands of black hair as she ascended the steps into the kitchen. "Is this a good time? Doris said she told you I would visit today." She glanced around as if making sure none of the children were within earshot then drew a stack of papers from her satchel. "I didn't only come to help with the decorations. I finished reading the pages you left with me last week. I thought we might go over my notes while Doris is out gathering flowers."

Hannah accepted the pages and promptly folded them in half so no one would see if they came into the room. Before she could reply, Doris sprang from the bedroom still wearing her bonnet, ran through the kitchen and into the parlor, and popped back into the kitchen, holding up a sea grass basket by its arched handle. "I found one!"

"Great," Olivia said. "Now remember to keep as much stem with the flowers as possible."

"Yes, Mrs. McIntosh." Doris smiled. Her eyes turned to Hannah. "I'll be in the meadow."

"Rain is coming."

"I won't be long."

The twins followed Doris outside, and Wade laced up his work boots to go start his barn chores. The folded pages warmed in Hannah's fingers as she waited for her brother to leave. She wanted to hear what Olivia thought of her evolving story. More than that, she wanted to tell Olivia her new goal. Though eager to begin their conversation, she wasn't about to give her youngest brother a hint of her private life, especially after the way David had behaved.

She motioned to the table for Olivia to take a seat. "Care for a cup of tea?"

"Only water for me, thanks."

Hannah set a covered plate on the table and peeled back a tea towel. "How about a sweet roll?"

Olivia's thin black eyebrows rose. "Icing? How delicious!" She selected one from the basket, took a bite, and hummed. "Thank heavens for sugar beets."

Hannah filled two cups with water and placed them on the table. She sat adjacent Olivia and unfolded her pages. A slight tremble vibrated Hannah's fingertips, so she tucked one hand into her lap. "Before we begin, I need to tell you something... to ask you something... your opinion about something."

Olivia leaned forward. "What is it?"

"My father knows I write. He's known about my story for years, and he wants to read it."

"Will you let him?"

Hannah pulled the scrunched notepaper from her apron pocket. She laid it on the table and smoothed out the wrinkles that had formed when David had teased her with it outside. If someone had mocked her about her notes, she dare not imagine what they would do with her story. "Not yet. I want it to be perfect first."

Olivia tilted her head a degree. "Will you let him read it once it's done?"

"Yes, but only because he asked. It seemed important to him. He spoke of getting older and not wanting to see me hide my talent. What do you think?"

"It's your decision."

"No, I mean, do you think my story will ever be good enough for someone else to read it?"

Olivia touched her hand. "I think it's good enough now. Overall, it just needs some polishing and a satisfying ending. You are the one who isn't pleased with it. Look through those pages and find my notes."

Hannah scanned the first page and flipped to the second then the third. The only marks on the page were hers. She continued searching for any of Olivia's usual editing marks but found none. "You didn't find any flaws in the entire chapter?"

Olivia shook her head and a silky strand of black hair escaped her chignon. "Your writing has matured. You have developed your characters beautifully. I was fascinated by the new plot you created for Adeline, and I'm eager to read the rest."

A strange sense of accomplishment mixed with terror gurgled inside her. "The rest," she repeated on a whisper.

"Do you know where the story is going now?"

She shook her head. "Not exactly."

"It's time to let your imagination take over. Use the talent God gave you."

"That's what my father said."

Olivia nodded. "He's right. You wanted my opinion. I believe you should finish your story and share it."

She held up a hand. "Only with my father for his birthday. I don't want anyone else to see it or even to know I write."

"When is his birthday?"

"In four months." She tapped her fingers on the papers. "Do you think I can finish in time?"

"Sure."

"And have time to make a copy for his gift?"

Olivia's eyes widened.

"What? You think that's impossible, don't you?"

"No, it's possible, but I have another idea." A mischievous grin made her dark eyes sparkle. "You should ask Henry Roberts to print and bind your story."

Hannah's stomach recoiled. "Like a book?"

"It isn't *like* a book, Hannah. It is a book. You're writing a novel."

"Yes, I know," she said without meaning it. She hadn't meant to write a book. It was a story—a story that kept her mind occupied during monotonous and lonely days, a story that allowed her to produce something bigger than laundry and dinner. It was still a story that never should be shared. It was part of her private world. "Henry probably doesn't have the time to print my little story."

Olivia shrugged. "It wouldn't hurt to ask. I think a bound, printed copy of your story would make a lovely gift for your father's fiftieth birthday."

"What if Henry says no?"

"Then you handwrite a copy."

"What if he tells everyone I write fiction?"

"Henry isn't like that."

If she finished her story and Olivia kindly edited it and Henry printed and bound it into a book, she would have succeeded in the goal she was putting before herself, but somehow success felt more dreadful than failure. If she failed to produce the story, there would be no book, no gift, no embarrassment, no torture of wondering what someone else thought of her words. But then she would be guilty of taking her talent to the grave. Scary as it was, she had to explore Olivia's idea. "What if Henry says yes?"

"Then you will have your manuscript turned into a book, and your father will be delighted."

Hannah stood and busied her hands at the stove. "No, I mean if Henry prints it, he will read it too."

"I'm sure he will enjoy the story."

"But what if he doesn't? Literature is subjective. You taught me that. You said readers perceive the story through the lens of their own experiences and preferences. What if Henry ridicules me? What if I can't write a strong ending?"

"Then I will tell you it needs more work before it is printed."

She had trusted Olivia with her story for six years. Olivia would stop her from sharing a story that wasn't fit to be read. But even if she finished the story and liked the ending and took it to Olivia and she approved of the story, she would have to trust Henry. Her simple pastime felt like ivy that began as a ground cover and was now blanketing the house, sucking the moisture from the wood. She turned back to face Olivia. "I'm not sure I can do this. I never wanted to be a published author."

Olivia tilted her head. "Then don't think of it as publishing a book but as making a present for your father. Henry and my husband have been friends their entire lives. He is trustworthy. Ask for his confidence in the matter and tell him I sent you." Olivia's playful grin returned. "He might not always be pleasant, but he will treat you fairly."

CHAPTER SIX

Henry chewed his cheek while waiting for the elders to slog through mind-numbing village business and get to his father's request to make the printing press a village-supported trade. The weekly Wednesday night elders' meetings always droned for hours, but tonight's agenda set a new standard for tedium. Henry's toes curled inside his boots as he fought the urge to blast out of his seat and beg Reverend Colburn to get to what mattered.

Sitting at Henry's left, his father shifted on the wooden pew. Matthew kept a stoic expression while Reverend Colburn opened the floor for the elders to discuss the use of the late Mr. Weathermon's cabin. Gabe McIntosh sat to Henry's right, smelling of sawdust after a day of building. Gabe crossed his arms when his father stood to speak.

"My son Arnold would like to have the empty cabin. Arnold plans to ask Hazel Roberts to marry soon. The cabin would suit them well."

There was a brief murmur between the men as discussion began. Gabe elbowed Henry and smirked. "My brother and your sister."

"Bound to happen," Henry mumbled, not amused.

The elders' discussion of Mr. Weathermon's old cabin didn't hold Henry's interest. His mind drifted and he cast his gaze to the window. The rain had stopped and the sun had long since set, but no stars were visible since the chapel interior's lamplight was reflecting off the glass.

Four large oil lanterns burned in the room. It seemed excessive, but ever since Dr. Ashton had found an efficient way to refine the oil he'd discovered in the shale down the coast, all the homes and workshops had brightened.

All except the print shop.

One spill of burning fuel could consume six months' worth of Henry's precious work. He would rather squint in candlelight than risk torching his exquisite pages. No matter what the genius Ashtons came up with, he would stick to candles. And as long as Hannah Vestal kept trading her candles for his paper, he was in no danger of wanting for light.

Hannah Vestal. He wanted to see her but didn't know why. It might be a long while before she came to trade again, considering the amount of paper she'd taken at once. Surely she was writing a novel to need so much paper at once. But she didn't behave like any writer he had known. Why had she acted secretively about needing paper? Maybe she wasn't a writer. The writers he knew back in America boasted about their craft as if the profession were an appointment so divinely bequeathed the populous would be destitute without them.

Hannah wasn't like those writers. She hadn't experienced a society that held the pursuit of fame in higher regard than the desire for holiness. She hadn't experienced much socializing at all but spent her life minding five siblings and her parents' home. Maybe the solitude had made her scared of people. Or of men. Or maybe she was just modest. Still, if she was a writer and her writing was any good, she wouldn't be secretive about it. Perhaps he should make a point of speaking with her after church on Sunday to see if she would divulge clues to her paper usage.

Beside him, Matthew stroked his white side whiskers while his gaze shifted between Mr. McIntosh and Reverend Colburn as the matter of Mr. Weathermon's cabin was brought to a vote. The reverend's dignified voice resounded through the narrow chapel. "All those in favor, say *aye*."

Matthew and the other elders replied, "Aye."

"Those opposed, say *nay*?"

No one objected.

Henry glanced at Gabe beside him then shot a look down the pew to Jonah. The three of them had spent eight years marveling at the elders' exhaustive discussions that usually ended in divided votes. Perhaps if the elders were feeling inclined to vote quickly and in the affirmative on Mr. McIntosh's request, they would be accommodating when the matter of the printing press was raised.

Reverend Colburn adjusted his slipping spectacles then silently read his notes at the lectern. Henry scratched the thickly scarred skin between his middle finger and the nub of his missing ring finger while the reverend followed the words he read with his pencil tip. What was taking him so long to read?

Finally, the reverend spoke, repeatedly glancing at his notes. "The Roberts family is making changes, or rather, Matthew has come to a decision about the occupations of his eldest two sons. Simon isn't suited for the work of the printing press but has taken over the family's farming while Matthew has devoted his time to making paper. He gave the printing press, including the workshop, to Henry. Of all this, I heartily approve as he is passing his primary vocation to his eldest son."

Since Henry was not allowed to speak up as a junior member in the council, he gave his father a light nudge. Matthew drew a trifolded square of scrap paper from his breast pocket and pinched the seam repeatedly between his fingers while he waited to be addressed.

Reverend Colburn continued speaking. "The occupation of printing and binding books to supply the school and church and to begin the village's library now falls to Henry, who has no home or land of his own with which to sustain himself. The Roberts family is pleased to allow Henry to remain at home and to provide him room and board for the time being. Like any man in Good Springs, once he decides to marry we would appoint him land and help him build a home." He removed his spectacles. "However, Mr. Roberts has proposed the village support Henry's livelihood continually by making the press a village-supported profession."

The reverend looked over the men seated in the first pew and settled his gaze on Matthew. "Have you prepared a statement?"

The elders in the front row craned their necks to look at Matthew. Henry tightened his abdominal muscles, bracing himself for his father's speech.

"I have." His father stood and straightened his lapel then unfolded his paper. "A pressman's life is defined by slow and precise work. Unlike the swinging of a hammer, the setting of type requires delicate perfection. The press's quiet heroism often goes unnoticed, unlike the often quick rescue of a physician."

Henry went back to chewing his cheek to refrain from groaning.

Matthew continued with his flowery monologue. "The work of the pressman benefits not one customer at a time but the village as a whole over time and, therefore, he should be supported by the village as a whole. The pressman's purpose in Good Springs is not simply to trade a product nor does the printing press exist solely to supply books to individuals for entertainment but for the furtherance of our education, for the guarantee that the Scripture won't be lost when our few Bibles fade, for the preservation of our culture from one generation to the next, the reinforcement of our values, the respite of the soul when swept into story, yea, for the enrichment of our very lives.

"As the village population doubles or triples every twenty years, the supply of Bibles and schoolbooks must increase, and that, men of Good Springs, takes the whole life of a committed pressman."

Several of the elders nodded in agreement, including Reverend Colburn.

Henry's toes relaxed inside his shoes. His father's eloquence appeared to have stirred the elders to approval.

"Thank you, Matthew," the reverend said. He looked at his notes and then at Henry. "Are you committed to this occupation for life, son?"

He stood beside his father and squared his shoulders. "I am." All that was left was arranging the terms of his support, and he could leave here a satisfied man.

Reverend Colburn patted the air, directing Henry to sit. Then he addressed the elders. "Is there a man among us who does not see the need and value of the printing press?"

No one spoke.

The reverend nodded. "Very well, Matthew you may be seated too. I recommend the village of Good Springs supports the livelihood of the pressman, not in perpetuity, only for Mr. Henry Roberts's lifetime and only under certain conditions."

His father hadn't mentioned the possibility of conditions. Henry swallowed air.

"First, we shall require proof of Henry's skill in the craft, especially his attention to detail, as the creation of no books would be preferable to error-filled texts. Second, since the nature of the work requires independence and persistence, we shall also require proof of Henry's ability to work skillfully and faithfully to see a project completed in a timed capacity. I know of no other way to test him than with an assignment. Henry, if you want the village to support the printing press, you must produce an error-free copy of the New Testament, printed and bound, by Good Springs's eighth anniversary celebration."

Henry's lips parted but before he could object, his father spoke. "Reverend, that is only four months away."

Reverend Colburn raised a palm, halting Matthew's protest. "If you don't believe it can be done, we will discuss other recommendations at a future meeting."

Henry would rather work twenty hours per day for four months than allow his livelihood be lost in council debates. He shot to his feet. "I can do it."

Matthew tugged on his sleeve, trying to make him sit.

What was he thinking? Only four months to print an error-free copy of the New Testament with no help, not even an ink boy? Every muscle in his body told him to recoil and pray his father could convince them to sponsor the press in the future, but he didn't budge. He looked Reverend Colburn in the eye. "I accept your terms, sir, should the elders agree."

The reverend nodded. "All in favor say *aye*."

Henry held his breath as he slowly lowered himself to the pew.

The elders responded in unison. "Aye."

"Those opposed say *nay*?"

When there was no response, the reverend pointed his pencil at Henry. "You have four months, son. I look forward to reading your work."

CHAPTER SEVEN

After helping Doris carry bundles of floral decorations to the school for the upcoming dance, Hannah dithered on the road in front of the bustling schoolhouse. She could turn south and walk to the print shop or turn north and go home. The print shop was nearby. What could it hurt to try?

She wanted to take Olivia's advice and ask Henry to print and bind her story if she finished it in time for her father's birthday. She'd gotten an early start on her cleaning chores this morning, and her father would support her if he knew what she was doing. There was no good reason for her hesitation. Still, she preferred standing on the road to choosing a direction.

Perhaps it was the comfort of the late spring sunlight glinting between the gray leaf trees overhead that beckoned her to stay put. Or maybe it was the soft morning air whispering through the village that gently immobilized her with its kind caress.

No, it was fear.

The same fear that made her hide her pages and keep her stories to herself. How could she write courageous characters that carried on despite their fear if she let fear strand her on the road between her safe home and the printer who might help her make a present for her father?

She was simply requesting Henry's services, not his opinion on her story. Olivia had assured her Henry would be fair, and she trusted Olivia. What was the worst that could happen? If Henry said no, she would have to give her father a handwritten copy of the story, which had been her original plan.

She rebuked her fear, stepped over a puddle left by yesterday's rain, and headed south.

Once near the print shop, she crossed the sandy gravel toward the log cabin that originally housed the Cotter family when they first arrived in the Land. The workshop's door stood ajar, and its window gaped at the mid-morning sun.

She stepped into the doorway. "Hello? Mr. Roberts? Henry?"

No one answered.

Her vision adjusted to the darkness in the vacant one-room workshop. The scents of copper and ink and man filled the space. The impeccably arranged shelves held little boxes of backward letters and stacks of paper, all arranged at perfect right angles.

She trailed a finger along the edge of the press and let her skin linger on the smooth polished wood of the ancient contraption. How many books had it printed in its lifetime? How many more volumes would come to life beneath its weight?

A half-page's worth of moveable type was nestled backward in rows on the letterpress. Henry must have been in the middle of setting type when he'd left. She looked closer. The top row read: *The Gospel According to Matthew.*

Her fingers itched to inspect the copper-plated letters and open the cabinet full of narrow drawers, but it would be rude to snoop. As she backed away from the letterpress, her elbow brushed a stack of pages on the worktable. She quickly straightened the pages and readjusted a paperweight atop the stack then stepped outside.

The empty road stretched through the woods to where her family's property capped the northern end of the village. Chimney smoke rose from the houses to the south, but no one was on the road. She walked to one end of the print shop and peeked around the corner. Only gray leaf trees waved from the woods that stood between the back of the building and the shore, so she walked to the other side. The outhouse door was closed, and she would not knock.

The stone facade of the recently built library next door commanded her attention. She'd seen inside only once—after the village's dedication ceremony—and that was for a quick look with her family. Other families had been waiting their turn to go in, and the twins had whined about being hungry, so she hadn't given the room a close inspection. The library had been empty then. Was it still?

Two sawhorses stood between the library and the print shop with a stack of lumber nearby. She padded across the sawdust-covered ground. The library's narrow wooden door had been constructed from the *Providence*'s deck planks and still smelled of seawater. A two-inch gap parted the door from its frame, so she pushed it farther open. The iron hinges creaked.

"Hello?"

Only a faint echo of her voice answered.

She stepped inside. Wooden bookshelves stretched from floor to ceiling around the perimeter of the library, save for one section of bare wall by the door. A plumb line hung from the top of the wall there, and a stack of tools rested near the baseboard. That must be what the lumber was for.

Her shoes scuffed along the stone floor as she perambulated the room. She couldn't remember ever having walked on such a smooth stone floor before. All the houses in the Land had wooden floors, as did her family's farmhouse back in Virginia. The stone gave the place a sacred feel, like the way she imagined the inside of a temple or mausoleum. Though as the town library, the hallowed air might warm once the shelves were filled with books.

A shadow darkened the doorway, and Henry stepped inside. He ran his right hand through his reddish brown hair and slid his left hand behind his back. "Miss Vestal?"

As he stared down at her from a foot taller, she tucked her chin. "So sorry to trespass."

His lips curved into a smile, but his brow creased with an authoritative scowl. "You aren't trespassing. This is a public building."

Her eyes met his and she almost looked away again, but something about the blue of them held her gaze. His scowl released and all that remained was a grin—charming with a hint of mischief. She mirrored his expression, hoping it might help her cause. "I've come to request your printing services."

"Ah." He folded his hands in front of his ink-stained leather apron but said nothing else.

"Upon Olivia's suggestion." Her voice echoed in the empty stone room, distracting her. "I can trade you candles or, if you prefer, apples from my father's orchard if you are willing to wait until autumn for payment."

He tilted his head as if asking for more explanation.

"It's my wish to make a present for my father's next birthday. It will be his fiftieth, you see, and he has made his desire known to me for a particular gift, so I will do my best to oblige."

"And that desire is what, Miss Vestal?"

"A book."

"What sort of book?"

"Fiction."

Henry lifted a palm. "Just any novel?"

"No, a specific story." She wet her dry lips. "Turning the story into a book is my idea... well it's Olivia's, actually. My father would like to read a story that I've written... that I am writing. Olivia is the only person other than my father who knows about my writing, and I must ask that you keep this matter private."

"Why?"

Air swooped into her lungs on a sharp inhale. She repeated his disrespectful question. "*Why?*"

"Yes, why do you believe writing a story to be a private matter?" His smile was gone. "In an isolated village as small as Good Springs, there are people praying for new stories to read. Did you ever consider them?"

"What? No. I mean, not that I don't consider others, but this is a private matter within my family." She lowered her voice to decrease the echo in the room. "I first read my story to my mother and now my father has asked to read it too. I'd like to present it to him on his birthday and do so without the entire village knowing of my pastime. Olivia thought it might be nice to have the story printed and bound for my father. I believe it would have made my mother proud."

At the mention of her mother, Henry's expression softened. He turned to the door and waved for her to follow him. They crossed the wet ground between the library and the print shop. He lit a candle on the worktable beside the press. "When is your father's birthday?"

"The fourteenth of March."

Henry wiped his face with both hands. "I have a very important project to finish by the twenty-first of March, which will take most of my waking hours between now and then."

"Oh." She dropped back a step, ready to leave him to his work. "Sorry to have bothered you. Thank you for your time."

"Has your story been edited?"

"It will be once it's finished."

"Once it's finished? But you said you had read the story to your mother."

She didn't need to be questioned, especially by some arrogant pressman who knew nothing about her story or her family or her private life. She marched toward the door then stopped abruptly to try one last time before leaving. "Will you print the story or not?"

"Not if it isn't finished."

Olivia had said Henry might not be pleasant but he would be fair. Hannah agreed about the unpleasant quality but had yet to witness his fairness. She whirled back around to face him. "How much time would you need for printing?"

"How many pages is it?"

She couldn't say without knowing how she would change the ending and what else might come to her in the process, but she wasn't about to give Henry Roberts those details. "About two hundred pages, handwritten."

"Thus your trade for paper the other day." He propped his left hand on his hip. The stumps from where he'd lost fingers formed a misshapen fist. "I'd need two weeks. No less." He lifted a little box of letters from the worktable and picked through them. "Will you have it finished and edited by the first of March?"

A tinge of hope warmed her heart. "So, you will print it? Name your price. Candles? Apples? I can bake, sew, make soap—"

"Candles." He lowered his chin, silencing her. "If you finish the story, not that I think you will, but if you do—"

She raised her voice. "Of course, I will finish it!"

"Of course, nothing." He flattened his tone. "If you have been revising it for six years, I lack faith in your ability to complete it in four months."

She straightened her spine, though it didn't increase her stature. "I will indeed finish the story for my father."

Henry shrugged as if unimpressed by her resolve. His fingers went back to riffling through the letters in the box, but his eyes moved from the letters to her and back. "Very well. Finish the story and bring it to me by the first of March. I must read it and consider it worthy of my press before I will agree to print it."

Every nerve in her skin bristled. "I only want your printing not your opinion. How dare you!"

He set the box down and spread both hands on his worktable. Leaning forward, he leveled his gaze on her. "It is not a matter of what I dare and dare not do, Miss

Vestal, as this is my press. I have very high standards of what I print. If I am to take the time to make the ink and set the type, not to mention the process of binding the book, I do indeed dare to first ensure the work deserves my expertise. If I find your story to be a noble literary work, I will print it. If it falls short of my standards in any way, I will not waste my ink."

She crossed her arms. "You don't think I could write a story worthy of your ink?"

"No."

"Why? Because I am female?"

"No, because you make no sense in your speech, causing me to doubt your ability to bring logic to the page. You want your writing kept secret, yet you want your story brought to press. You consider the story unfinished, yet you read the completed story to your mother…" His voice lost its force when he spoke of her mother. He rubbed the palm of his scarred hand. "Since out of sentiment you're determined to have it printed, I will read the finished work—if you can indeed finish it. If I deem it worthwhile, I will print and bind it for you… for your father. If not, you must accept my decision as one of business. It's nothing personal, Miss Vestal. Try your best not to take offense."

"Not to take offense?" A strong retort dissolved on her tongue. If his main concern with her ability to write was because he found her words lacked logic, arguing out of anger might only solidify his opinion. She took a slow breath and steadied her voice. "Thank you for your consideration. I will deliver the finished and edited manuscript to you before the first of March." She stepped to the door allowing the air to cool her burning cheeks. Before walking away, she glanced back. "You are incorrect about one thing, though, Mr. Roberts. I bring logic to the page by empowering my stories first with emotion. Anyone who possesses the slightest insight into the human experience would appreciate the tension in my reasoning."

Henry's eyes widened, but in a fraction of a second he erased the surprise from his face. His faintly mischievous grin returned. "Good day, Miss Vestal."

"Good day, Mr. Roberts."

CHAPTER EIGHT

The sun sank behind the trees to the west, lining
cumulous clouds with splotches of orange light. As
Henry neared his workshop, he sucked on one of the hard
candies his mother had set out in a glass dish after dinner.
She'd made them with licorice, saying his favorite flavor
would bring him comfort while he worked long into the
night. Having his family's encouragement empowered his
determination to meet the elders' challenge and secure
village support for the printing press.

He reached for the doorknob but stopped short before
he turned it. Something was amiss. When he had pulled
the door closed before he left for dinner, he'd turned the
knob a quarter to the left so a dark knot in the wood
would be in the noon position. It was an old habit he'd
started when he was young and his sisters enjoyed
snooping in his room while he was gone. Once the print
shop was his, he'd found a mark in the doorknob's wood
and positioned it precisely every time he left the shop.

He switched the candy to the other side of his mouth
and glanced over his shoulder. Light glowed through the
shuttered window of the library next door. A hammer's

muted pound thudded rhythmically. Gabe was finishing the bookshelves.

The chapel across the road was dark, as was the schoolhouse. No one was on the road in either direction.

Henry cracked open the door and peered into his workshop before stepping inside. The pages he'd left hanging to dry quivered in the air that blew through the open doorway. Nothing else moved, but the blackness of the shadows behind the press had him reaching into his trouser pocket.

His fingers curled around his closed pocketknife just as his tongue curled around the candy. His heart thumped against the wall of his chest. He drew the knife from his pocket. What was he thinking? He wouldn't stab a person. If anyone were in his shop, he or she would be a member of the community, possibly a child. He knew what it was like to have flesh ripped, and he'd never inflict that pain upon another individual.

He dropped the knife back into his pocket and took out a match instead. Striking it, he stepped inside and lit one of the candles he'd received in trade with Hannah.

As the flame spread upon the wick, he lowered the candle into a mirrored lantern then circled the room. He was alone, but someone had been here. A folded scrap of paper perched like a tent on his worktable. His name was scribbled in pencil on the note's exterior. He unfolded it and read its one sentence: *stay Away from hannah Vestal*.

He looked at the windows, the open door, and back toward the unsigned note. Who would write such a message?

The writing's quick slant and straight stems proved a masculine hand, ruling out the females in the village. Besides, he couldn't imagine any woman in Good

Springs writing a note like this. He'd hurt Cecelia Foster's feelings last year, but her anger had since cooled.

So the note's writer had to be a male. The mismatched usage of upper and lower case suggested a lack of education. That ruled out all the elders. So a young man must have written the note.

He flipped the paper over and rubbed a thumb along the deep pencil grooves. Whoever had written this was upset when he wrote it. But who?

He thought back to his visit from Hannah earlier in the day. She had made a point of asking for privacy, so it was doubtful she told anyone about the meeting. He couldn't recall seeing or hearing anyone else on the road at the time, but he hadn't been paying close attention. He'd been focused on beginning the New Testament project for the elders, and when Hannah came in, he'd been struck by a mixture of annoyance and intrigue.

Why would her coming to him with a business request infuriate any young man in the village?

The hammering stopped in the library next door. Henry folded the note and slid it into his shirt pocket as Gabe came into the workshop. He raised his chin at Gabe. "Done for the night?"

Gabe grinned. "Done for good. Shelves are up."

"Did you see anybody come in here while I was gone?"

"No. Why?"

"Just curious."

Gabe pointed a thumb toward the library. "I'll clean up and get my tools tomorrow."

Henry nodded then checked the ink on the pages hanging up to dry behind the worktable. "Does Hannah Vestal have a suitor?"

"Not to my knowledge."

"She and Olivia are friends, aren't they?"

Gabe stepped to the other side of the worktable and pinched the edge of one of the wet pages. "They've been friends for years... since Mrs. Vestal died. Olivia helps Hannah with her writing."

"So you know about Hannah's writing."

Gabe held up both hands in surrender. "And it's between them. My wife tells me very little about Hannah's visits, and I don't ask questions." He motioned to the printed pages hanging from the line. "You think you can do this?"

"Do what?"

"Meet the elders' challenge. Print an error-free copy of the New Testament in four months."

Henry had run the numbers twice. He had the paper, the ingredients for the ink so long as people brought him soot, and the determination. "If nothing happens to the press and I'm able to focus on only this task, I should have it done in time. I'll have to work every night, but I don't mind."

Gabe pointed at the candle. "Oil lanterns would be brighter."

"I don't want fuel in here. One fiery spill and I could lose all of my work."

"I suppose your mother is happy to make the extra candles for you."

"Wasn't my mother's doing." Henry turned to the press so Gabe wouldn't see his face. "Hannah traded them for paper."

Gabe smirked. "Hannah?"

"Yes."

"That's why you wanted to know if she has a suitor."

Henry ignored the ache simmering inside his chest and drew the unsigned note from his pocket. He passed it to Gabe. "No. This was."

Gabe frowned as he read it. "Who is it from?"

Henry shrugged. "Someone entered my shop while I was at dinner. They left it on my worktable."

"Show it to Olivia. She will know whose handwriting it is."

"I'd rather forget about it. Hannah would be embarrassed if the matter came to light."

Gabe refolded the note and handed it back. "It might not be bad advice."

"What?"

"To stay away from her... romantically. Don't forget what happened with Cecelia."

The mention of Cecelia made the ache in Henry's chest expand. Was it his fault he didn't have the patience for women, that they were so easily offended, that he preferred the quiet of his workshop to the incessant chatter of insecure girls who demanded constant attention?

So what if Hannah was different, complex, intriguing? He was done with putting his heart at risk for women who didn't understand him. He held up his left hand to stop the conversation. It worked on everyone. "Believe me, I am not interested in Hannah Vestal."

CHAPTER NINE

A violin's melodious hum floated on the wind as Hannah accompanied Doris to the spring dance at the schoolhouse. The stiff edges of Hannah's new dress shoes pressed into her ankles as Doris hurried them along. She reached for Doris's arm. "No need to rush. We aren't late."

"The music has started."

"Mr. Cotter is probably warming up."

Doris craned her neck. "If Sarah gets there first, Benjamin will ask her to dance and not me." She pointed through the waning twilight at the lamp-lit schoolhouse. "See, we're late."

Hannah let go of her arm. "Slow down. We don't want to arrive red-faced and out-of-breath."

"Everyone else is already there."

"We would have been here sooner if you hadn't insisted I wear curls."

Doris flashed her a playful smile. "I had to. You've been looking dowdy lately."

Hannah's iron-formed curls bounced around her face as she and Doris trotted to the schoolhouse. She pushed the curls off her forehead, but they sprang back into place thanks to the floral-scented pomatum Doris had borrowed from Sarah Ashton. Dowdy or not, she never should have let Doris talk her into such frivolity.

Doris dashed ahead of her, climbing the schoolhouse steps in time with the music's quick beat. Hannah hurried, not wanting her young sister to enter without a chaperone. The music's volume rose as the door opened. A drum and mandolin joined the jolly tune.

The desks and chairs had been removed, leaving the long schoolroom void of seating and open for dancing and mingling. Doris's flowery decorations adorned the walls at regular intervals. Young people danced in a formal circle while their chaperones—mostly older siblings—flanked the schoolhouse walls. The stuffy room already smelled of sweat and anxious adolescents.

It was the village custom for all attendees to dance at least once to show a good spirit. Hannah dearly loved to dance but doubted she'd be asked. She enjoyed watching people more than dancing, and there was plenty to observe.

She leaned close to Doris's ear and raised her voice over the music. "Your decorations look beautiful. Well done!"

Doris smiled then stood on her tiptoes. "Anthony is playing the drum. Isn't he handsome?"

She chuckled at her starry-eyed sister. "I thought you were hoping Benjamin would ask you to dance tonight."

"Either one." Doris giggled then nudged Hannah. "It appears you have an admirer."

Hannah scanned the crowd of young people and chaperones. "Who?"

Doris shielded her mouth with a gloved hand. "Henry Roberts."

She followed Doris's line of sight to Henry. He stood near the dance floor with one hand casually in his trouser pocket and the other hand smoothing the back of his coppery brown hair. When their gaze met, a mixture of aggravation and attraction wrestled inside her. She looked away. "He's probably here as Ellenore's chaperone."

"He's been watching you since we walked in. You should talk to him."

"I will not."

"He is a dapper sort of fellow. I'll talk to him."

"You will do no such thing." She pinched the back of Doris's arm. "He's twice your age."

Doris giggled again then dashed off to join her friends. The girls she was so worried about competing with fawned over her dress and petted her puffed sleeves.

Hannah glanced around the room for an empty spot along the wall where she might take refuge. Voices swelled as the dancers laughed and the observers shouted to keep their conversations alive over the music. Reverend Colburn stood beneath one of the flower wreaths at the head of the classroom, looking as if he'd rather be anywhere else in the Land. Hannah understood the feeling but couldn't pass up this opportunity to glean inspiration for her story.

Her brother David stood across the room with some of the village's older boys. They weren't boys anymore but young men; many of them were in training with their fathers to one day be village elders, but for tonight they were young men perusing a spring dance, hopeful to catch the eye of a young lady.

What if Prince Aric were in a similar situation when he first noticed Adeline? What if instead of the drab scene where he meets Adeline on the road, they meet at a ball? A masquerade? She might be in borrowed clothes or trying to disguise herself to slip through the palace and he mistakes her for a courtier. Or maybe she's working the ball as a servant, picks up a lost mask, and he thinks she is one of them. No, mistaken identity was used too frequently in romantic tales. The test of Aric's love should be in committing to a commoner against his parents' wishes, not in finding reasons to love her after being deceived.

But, oh, what it must be like to fall in love at a dance!

Perhaps the power of the story was in the perspective. Maybe Adeline should first notice Aric at a ball, but he doesn't notice her. She could spend days thinking about him, fantasizing scenarios of meeting him, being courted by him, captivating him.

Hannah hummed aloud unintentionally. No one could have heard her over the music, but her cheeks warmed. She started to walk toward the door for fresh air when someone tapped her on the shoulder.

Henry's brother Simon smiled, his thick lower lip curving more than the upper. "Would you care to dance, Miss Vestal?"

He'd been two years ahead of her in school back in Virginia, but he'd only stayed through the sixth grade. She remembered him being kind but not particularly smart. Since she had to dance with someone, Simon Roberts would make a harmless partner. She accepted the arm he offered. "Yes, thank you."

As they joined the circle of waiting couples in the center of the room, her gaze fell on Henry who remained near the dance area with his left hand still in his pocket even though there were plenty of young ladies not yet dancing. His light blue eyes shot a contemptuous stare at Simon.

What right have he to be displeased by his brother's choice of dancing partner? First, he'd asserted himself into her writing process by saying he'd only print her story if he approved of it, and now he scowled at his brother for dancing with her. Though her feet followed the rhythmic steps of the dance and her face offered a friendly smile to her partner, she thought only of Henry's audacity until the dance was over.

When the song ended with a triple beat from the drum and a soft note fading from the violin, the dancers applauded each other and the musicians. With a quick nod of thanks to Simon, Hannah left the dancers to their sweaty circle and made haste to the door.

The cool air lapped the heat from her skin. Her gloved hand hovered over the wooden rail as she descended the schoolhouse steps. As soon as the door closed and she was alone, she removed her gloves and loosened her starched collar. Without pins, there was nothing she could do to keep the stiff curls off her forehead. Tomorrow she'd pay in blemishes for tonight's primping.

And all for what? One dance.

She wasn't here for herself but for her sister. Doris was getting the adolescence Hannah never had. Perhaps as a bystander in Doris's upbringing she could experience enough youthful preening and romantic angst to write young love adequately. Perhaps not.

Maybe her story wasn't meant to be a love story at all but only a tale of missed experience and distant observation.

The music pulsed to life again inside the schoolhouse, and the door rattled as the dancers bobbed and the crowd shifted. Hannah ambled around the side of the building to where the school desks and chairs had been banished. The chairs were too low to the sandy ground to keep her full skirt out of the sand while sitting, so she hoisted herself upon a desk.

Her new shoes dangled above the earth. As she leaned her head back to take in the stars and the bright oval-shaped moon, footsteps swished over the sand and gravel at the front of the building. She held still, hoping not to draw attention to the restful place she'd found.

A shadow rounded the schoolhouse. "Did my brother's poor dancing chase you away?"

She didn't have to see his face to know Henry was smirking, but she flicked a glance at him anyway. "Not at all. Simon is quite amiable."

He slid a finger along his collar and opened the knot in his cravat. "Stuffy in there."

"Indeed." She returned her attention to the stars above, hoping Henry would take the hint and go away. He didn't move. Why wasn't he walking away?

After a quiet moment, he took a step closer. "I like your curls."

She pushed her hair off her forehead. "Doris insisted. She's quite girlish. It's nonsensical."

"It's pretty. You look like your mother."

At that, her gaze peeled away from the sky. "Thank you."

Just as the kindness of his comment sank in and almost softened her heart toward him, he asked, "Are you interested in Simon?"

She was not, but if she were, it wouldn't be any of Henry's business. Tonight, many couples would dance who had no romantic interest in each other. How was her dance with Simon any different? "Why do you ask?"

"I saw you together. You looked like you were enjoying yourself."

His assumptions made her jaw clench. If she were interested in his brother, would he object to them courting as he'd objected to printing her manuscript? First her book wasn't good enough for his ink, and now she wasn't good enough for his brother. She narrowed her eyes at him. "I enjoy dancing, and Simon was polite enough to ask. I won't let your brother court me, if that is what you're worried about."

His arrogant brow creased. "Did I offend you?"

She scooted off the desktop. "I should go back inside. I'm here as Doris's chaperone."

"She's in a chatty huddle with Sarah Ashton and Roseanna Colburn. The reverend hasn't taken his eyes off them." He slid both hands into his pockets. "How have I offended you?"

"Pardon?"

"Why are you upset with me?"

Though it might have been the moonlight affecting his expression, his eyes held sincerity. Could he be unaware of his haughty demeanor and prickly tone? Perhaps Prince Aric would also benefit from such a flaw, however, a lack of charm might make Adeline less attracted to him.

Maybe Henry's disinclination to polish his harsh opinions had more to do with sincerity than pride. She wouldn't find out by walking away, and she owed it to her writing to investigate. She leaned back against the desk and crossed her arms over her bodice. "You said I couldn't write a story worth printing."

He drew both hands out of his pockets and crossed his arms, reflecting her posture. "I explained that was a business decision. My father taught me long ago not to print every manuscript presented to me. There's no reason for you to be angry with me. If it were your press, wouldn't you use discernment in deciding what to print?"

"You judged my writing unprintable without reading it."

Someone stepped outside. They both glanced toward the front of the building. A shadow lingered at the front of the building but no one came into view.

When Henry looked back at her, he spoke with a quieter voice. "I said I would read it and make my decision then. I was simply letting you know the potential outcome. Isn't that better than if I had pretended to anticipate enjoying your story only to refuse to print it?"

She sucked in an incredulous breath. "See, you assume my story won't be enjoyable. It's your prejudice that offends me."

"My honesty offends you."

"You're conceited."

"You're illogical."

She jabbed the air with a finger. "I will shape my story into such a powerfully moving novel, you will choke on your tears when you read it."

Henry drew his head back and widened his eyes. She lowered her pointing finger, unsure of why she'd become so angry. Folding her hands loosely, she glanced around to see if anyone else had witnessed her outburst. They were alone unless someone was around the corner on the schoolhouse steps.

She focused on the shadowed ground around her feet. "I'm sorry."

"Never apologize for defending your work." His voice had lost its edge. "When you seemed ashamed of your writing, I didn't want to read it, but this passion has awakened my curiosity."

She studied his face. What he lacked in charm, he made up for in honesty. Perhaps this was the fairness Olivia had spoken of. If he took his work so seriously as to judge what he printed, maybe she could trust him with her story. Still, the thought of someone besides Olivia reading her work brought a sickly ache to her belly. "This is unnerving for me."

He leaned in a degree. "What is?"

Though no one else was near, she lowered her voice to barely above a whisper. "My mother was the only person I shared my writing with. After she died, Olivia understood how I felt. She helped my family, and I trusted her. Now my father says he wants to read my story, so I'm finishing it. Olivia suggested I have it printed, and that meant coming to you. I only came to you because I trust her. I know you have standards for your press, and you know nothing about my writing, but I don't know you. Not really. Not well enough to be comfortable with you reading my story and making judgments."

Henry gazed down at her for a quiet moment. He uncrossed his arms and rubbed the palm of his scarred hand with the thumb of the other. "I suppose you miss your mother very much."

She'd grown used to receiving the look of sympathy but didn't expect it from him. Not now. "Yes, I do."

"I can only imagine what that must have been like. I was very sorry for you and your family when she died. Still am."

"That is kind of you."

"Has the grief lessened with time?"

"A little. The sting has worn off, but the ache is persistent."

He looked down at his left hand. "I know the feeling."

"I miss her. That's part of the reason I write. Characters are good company."

His half-smiling half-scowling expression returned. "That doesn't make sense."

"Never mind." She began to cross her arms again, ready for another argument, but he caught her fingertips in his hand. Inside the schoolhouse, the muffled drum counted off a beat and a slower song began.

His face changed and he lifted her hand. "Would you care to dance, Miss Vestal?"

"Thank you, but I don't want to go back inside yet."

"I too prefer the space and fresh air out here." His grin reached his eyes. "It's tradition that everyone must dance at least once to show a good spirit. I have a good spirit but no dance partner."

She smiled and mocked a quick curtsy. "I wouldn't want to hinder your efforts in upholding the tradition, sir."

He chuckled. "Then dance with me." Still grinning, he placed his left hand on the small of her back and held her hand with his right. "You shall not regret it."

She lightly touched his shoulder, keeping her elbow up, as he led the dance across the sandy soil. Stray blades of grass tickled her skin as her skirts swished over the ground. Hopeful starlight shone around them, and the music spilled through the schoolhouse wall. With each pulse of the third beat, their feet rotated the box step movement. Gravel crackled underfoot, but the uneven turf was no match for his confidence.

Perhaps there was more to Henry Roberts than she'd realized.

All at once, her story flooded her mind. The solution to her plot problem was not in how Adeline met Prince Aric, but in why. Details of the air, the sky, the scents of ocean and earth swam through her imagination. Her characters' faces were as crisp as anyone she knew, as were their hopes and needs and wounds.

Everything she'd been trying to force in her story fell away as she danced with Henry in the darkened schoolyard. It was as if the sudden reality of this new experience permeated the fictional world that lurked beneath the surface of her mind, making both equally real to her at once. One reality she could touch and smell, but the other might dissolve into nothingness if she didn't concentrate on memorizing every detail. Why hadn't she brought a pencil and paper?

If she kept Adeline and Aric's faces before her mind and the fulfillment in their hearts as they came together, she would remember it all when she was able to write later tonight. While she focused on her characters' world, the energy of the surrounding reality slipped and took the joy of the fictive dream with it. Somehow she had to concentrate on both the world around her and the world inside her mind.

Listening to the music, their footsteps, and Henry's breath as he led the dance, she absorbed the warmth of his hand on her back, the sureness in his movements, and the palpable tension between them. Her eyes closed and she envisioned Adeline and Aric meeting, loving, hating, needing, protecting themselves and each other, fighting, giving up, and finally giving in.

It was all there somehow mixed in the reality flowing around her and the story coming to life within her. It was as though none of it existed but all of it had always been, and somehow it was because of Henry Roberts.

Henry held Hannah's soft hand in his and led their moonlit dance across the sandy yard. As he stepped in time with the music that bled through the north wall of the schoolhouse, his mother's dance instructions echoed in his mind. *Keep your partner close enough to feel your movement but not so close as to seem improper.* That hadn't been a problem when he was being taught to dance in the parlor of their home and his sisters had been his partners. This was different.

Hannah smelled like flowers and soap, and her body heat warmed his palm. Could she feel the difference in his hand—nubs instead of the last two fingers? Was she thinking about it? Repulsed by it?

She was a delicate young woman, lonely and overworked, who missed her mother. She was also a passionate writer who bubbled with ideas and insecurities. And for some reason, she'd agreed to dance with him.

She'd also danced with his half-wit of a brother, so maybe she simply enjoyed dancing, just as she'd claimed.

Maybe this meant nothing to her. And it shouldn't mean anything to him no matter if he felt more hope and happiness than he had in years. Feelings couldn't be trusted. That's why God gave man logic to corral wayward feelings.

Still, he felt something irrepressible.

Why should he feel anything? She was only allowing him one dance. Even if she learned to keep her illogical jabbering to herself, he wouldn't ask her for more than this one dance. He couldn't. If he tried to get to know her, he wouldn't like her. If he found himself loving her, he'd only hurt her. Women were too sensitive, too irrational.

The unease and longing he felt was rooted in pity, perhaps even sympathy. He'd witnessed her at her mother's burial years ago and still felt the weight of tragedy when he saw her. She deserved to be loved by someone who would protect her and not ruin her. He was too harsh for such a fragile creature.

Her hand was warm in his, her skin smooth, unscarred. She was far too sweet to find him anything but caustic. He didn't need the scrutiny of another woman. He had tried before. They were all the same. Smiles and shy glances led to demands and crying.

And then there were the demands he placed on himself for what he could not give a woman. The unreliable strength in his scarred hand wouldn't allow him to build or farm or hunt the way the other men did.

The song ended, and their feet stilled on the sandy soil. He loosened his grip, but Hannah didn't let go of his hand. She opened her eyes and looked up at him. He hadn't realized she'd closed them. She hadn't simply danced with him; she had trusted him.

The hand he'd held against her back hovered there, barely touching the fabric of her dress. He didn't want to trap her but felt less inclined to pull away with every second she stayed near. Why was this private and beautiful woman not retreating from him?

There were certainly more handsome men, more prosperous. He was an impaired printer with eight ink stained fingers. He had smirked at her trade requests and scoffed at her talent, yet she hadn't fled. Even now, without music or provocation, she stayed close and had yet to let go.

He hoped she never would.

He studied her starlit features from her high cheekbones to the shadowed dip above her mouth, trying to memorize every line and curve in case he never saw her like this again. After a long moment, he lowered their joined hands. "Thank you, Miss Vestal."

Her words flowed out on a breath. "It was my pleasure."

Her gaze flicked to his mouth, but he denied the urge to wet his lips. Every fiber in his being yearned to kiss her, but he had no right. Though attracted, even intrigued by Hannah Vestal, he didn't love her enough to offer the kind of commitment she would expect after a kiss. However, he did love her enough as a neighbor—and maybe even as a friend—to protect her from himself.

He watched her lips as he pulled away. She gave no hint of wanting to be kissed, but her unmoving stance seemed like an invitation. Though he should have moved back, his body refused. How had she entranced him with a look?

The schoolhouse door opened again. Voices and lamplight flooded out. Hannah promptly let go of his hand and clasped her wrists in front of her. "Good evening, Mr. Roberts," she said as she turned and strode back into the schoolhouse.

CHAPTER TEN

Hannah set her pencil on the kitchen table and rubbed the cramp that had formed between her thumb and forefinger. Two hours straight of writing was good for the soul but bad for the hands. She leaned her head against the top slat of the ladder-back chair and closed her fatigue-laden eyes. It was too early in the afternoon to be this tired, but that's what she got for staying up late to write every night for a week.

The twins' muffled voices mixed with her father's and Doris's outside as they approached the house. Hannah hid her pages under a tea towel and tied on her apron. Her father opened the back door and her three sisters stepped into the mudroom. The quiet kitchen filled with the cacophony of family.

"Those are my shells!" Minnie yelled, as she grabbed at the seashells in Ida's cupped hands.

"Now, girls, we gathered plenty for you to share," Christopher said in an authoritative but kind tone. "Doris, help them take the shells to the parlor, please."

Hannah followed her squabbling sisters. She knelt on the parlor rug and picked dried seagrass out of Minnie's curls. "How was your time at the beach?"

"We saw a jellyfish!" Ida squealed.

"I hope you didn't touch it." She looked through the kitchen at Christopher. "Did you catch anything for dinner?"

Her father was still on the stoop, shaking the sand out of his cuffs. He held up a line with several fresh fish hanging from it and winked at her.

Doris pulled more shells out of Minnie's dress pocket. "You should have come with us, Hannah. It was lovely."

"Quite so." Christopher walked inside, wearing the red wool socks Hannah had knitted for him last Christmas. She'd planned to make everyone in the family a new pair of socks for Christmas again this year. With only a month until the holiday, she needed to start knitting soon.

Her father squeezed her shoulder with a sandy hand. "Did you enjoy your afternoon alone?"

"Quite so." She repeated him then glanced out the window. "Where are David and Wade?"

"Went to play cards with the Ashton boys. They'll be back in time for dinner."

"Cards? On a Sunday?"

Christopher turned to the cabinet and took out a boning knife. "What does Sunday have to do with playing cards?"

"Seems sacrilegious."

Christopher flashed her a grin. "You've read that book from Olivia with the medieval tales too many times, haven't you?"

"I suppose so." Hannah glanced at the table where her freshly written pages were hiding beneath the towel. "Since the girls are occupied and you are frying fish for dinner, would you mind if I go out for a while?"

Christopher grinned. "To go to the springs to write?"

"No, I'm done writing for the day," she whispered. "I'd like to ride Zelda over to Olivia and Gabe's house. I wanted to ask Olivia to read my new pages," she lifted her chin toward the parlor where the girls were arguing over the seashells, "without a crowd."

He nodded. "Of course. Biscuits with dinner?"

"Already made a batch." With renewed vigor, she gathered her papers from the table and stuffed them in her old school satchel. Slinging the strap over her shoulder, she pulled on her boots then grabbed a rope from a hook by the back door.

She hurried toward the pasture, hoping to harness her favorite of the family's two horses and saddle the mare in the barn before any of her siblings saw her preparing to leave. Zelda stood beneath a gray leaf tree, eating grass. The horse's brown and white mane parted revealing her big black eyes. When the mare spotted Hannah, she trotted toward the fence, flies swarming about her grassy mouth. Though the horse belonged to the family, she thought of Zelda as hers.

She led Zelda into the hay-scented barn to be brushed and saddled, talking all the while. No one was outside. Still, she kept her voice quiet. "I made all the changes to my story—everything that came to mind after the dance last week. Adeline's character is much stronger now, as is the plot. Instead of meeting Prince Aric by accident and falling in love, now she is on a mission. After being shipwrecked on a sandbar, our heroine swims to shore, escaping her captors. She finds her way to the palace to tell the king about being taken by force from her homeland and how the slave traders have been terrorizing her country.

"Adeline intends to ask the king to help her return to her homeland, but as she is telling him about the slave traders and the atrocities she witnessed aboard their vessel, she feels compelled to ask him not only to help her but also to command his navy to patrol the sea to stop the rash of kidnappings."

Hannah tightened the leather saddle straps then led Zelda out of the barn and hoisted herself onto the horse. "The intoxicated king refuses Adeline's request, saying she is a servant girl who has gone mad. He dismisses her from court. While the guards are escorting her to the gates, a prince is riding toward the palace, flanked by soldiers and wearing royal attire. Adeline begs him to hear her. The prince stops the guards and allows Adeline to tell her story. At first, she expects the prince to be just like his father, but he believes her. Prince Aric introduces himself and says he can take her to a safe place. He offers his hand to pull her onto his horse, and they ride off to a monastery."

Hannah stopped talking as she rode Zelda past the house. She held both reins loosely in one hand and petted Zelda's smooth hair with the other. Being on her horse was almost as freeing as writing. Once they were on the road, she gently kicked Zelda, sending her into a trot. "We made it past our own palace guards, Zee."

They were alone on the tree-lined road. Afternoon sunrays seeped between the gray leaf trees overhead, highlighting the dust that swam in the air. With no one around, she imagined she was an emissary racing between European villages with a secret delivery. Zelda's hoofbeats clopped the road with urgency.

Hannah glanced at the Roberts' house as she passed and was instantly snapped out of her fantasy. Mrs. Roberts was sitting on the front porch, so Hannah waved and wondered if Henry were home. Surely he wouldn't be working at the press on a Sunday, though he'd said his current project would take all of his waking hours for months.

She wanted to see him again. After the dance last week, she'd been filled with inspiration. The creative energy had yet to wane, and she already wanted more. Why had their dance given her a jolt of inspiration?

At first, she'd thought doing something different somewhere different with someone new had brought it on, but it was more than that. Being alone with Henry outside at night had brought a sense of secrecy, intimacy even, that she'd never experienced before. They had been in the midst of Good Springs, surrounded by their community yet hidden.

Beyond secrecy, the fire that burned during their quarrel had changed the moment Henry took her hand. The simple, sweet gesture meant nothing and everything all at once. Surely he wasn't intrigued with her; he acted like he found her impetuous. And she certainly wasn't intrigued with him. He was proud and harsh and spent way too much time with his precious letterpress.

Still, she thought about Henry as she rode into the village and turned by the chapel to follow the path to Olivia's house. She slowed Zelda's pace so they could enjoy the beauty of the woods that led down toward the big stream. Before they reached the water, the house Gabe had built for Olivia years ago came into view. With its painted door, stately gables, and cutaway shutters, it looked like something out of a story book.

Gabe was in the yard tossing a baseball with their three-year-old. Little Daniel looked like the perfect blend of his parents. He had Olivia's straight black hair and Gabe's dimpled smile.

"Hello," she called to them as she pulled on the reins, stopping Zelda.

Gabe handed the ball to Daniel then smiled at Hannah. "Good afternoon, Miss Vestal."

She swung down from the saddle and pointed at Daniel. "He's good at playing catch."

"We're working on his pitch." Gabe chuckled and took the reins. "I'll tie Zelda up by the barn. Olivia is in the house. You can go in."

As she opened the door, she could hear the rhythmic thuds of a butter churn. A pot of venison stew sweetened the air. A leaning stack of Daniel's wooden toy blocks adorned the parlor floor.

"Shoes off, young man!" Olivia called out before she looked up from the churn. "Oh sorry, Hannah. I thought Daniel was coming inside again."

"Is this a bad time?"

"Not at all." Olivia released the plunger and wiped her sweaty forehead with a handkerchief. "I was hoping you would come to visit soon."

Hannah opened her satchel and drew out the freshly written pages. "I had a burst of creative energy this week and completely rewrote the first half of the story. I'm thrilled with where the plot is going."

Olivia drew her head back and smiled. "I don't believe I've ever heard you say that."

"Something has changed. I truly feel like this is the story I was meant to tell." She fidgeted once her hands were empty. Her fingertips tingled with misplaced excitement. "You don't have to read it right now. I need to get home before dinner. I was just so happy about the story, I had to share it with you."

Olivia pressed the papers to her chest. "Well, I'm looking forward to reading it." She tilted her head. "Would this new inspiration have anything to do with Henry Roberts?"

Hannah hadn't told anyone about the private dance they had shared and was sure they had gone unseen. How could Olivia know? Had Henry been intrigued? Maybe he told Gabe who told Olivia? Did the whole village know about their dance? It was an inspiring moment and maybe romantic, but she wasn't intrigued with him. She tried to keep her expression neutral but her face warmed. "Whatever do you mean?"

"Having the story printed and bound for your father's birthday. Did you go to ask Henry about it?"

"Oh, that." A nervous chuckled escaped her throat. "Yes, I did."

"Well?"

She shrugged one shoulder. "He said he would have to read it first. If he approves of the story, he will print it in exchange for candles."

"If he approves?" Olivia chortled. "That's our Henry."

"I cringe at the thought of him reading it."

"Try not to worry about the future. It certainly won't help today. I'm proud of you for going to him. That had to be difficult for you." She nestled the papers into a writing box atop her desk then closed the box and patted it. "I'll keep your pages safe until I can read them."

"Thank you."

"It will take longer than usual for me; you wrote a great deal in a week."

"I've never been so inspired in all my life."

"Hold onto whatever sparked that inspiration for as long as you can."

Hannah's eyes felt heavy. She yawned and covered her mouth. "I will but I cannot keep writing so late at night—into the morning hours really—not with the children and the house to take care of."

"I understand. During the school year, I'm often grading papers from when Daniel goes to bed until midnight."

"How do you find time for everything?"

"It's a matter of sticking to your priorities and knowing when to ask others for help. Gabe often takes care of Daniel in the evenings so I can get housework done." Little Daniel smacked the back door, trying to push it open. Olivia flashed Hannah a grin as she went to let her son into the kitchen. "Of course, it doesn't always work out like I hope. Maybe things will be different for you."

CHAPTER ELEVEN

Henry paced to the print shop's open door for the third time this morning. Mr. Foster had promised that by nine o'clock he would deliver the soot he'd collected. Henry held a clay pint jar full of walnut oil and gave it a stir as he leaned out the doorway to check the road.

There was plenty of activity in the village for a Friday morning, but no Mr. Foster. Mrs. Colburn was walking to the chapel with her three youngest children in tow. She had a tin lunch pail dangling by the handle from her lace-cuffed wrist. Mr. Owens drove his buckboard past. One squeaky wheel joint begged for grease. Mr. Owens nodded a greeting to Henry as his horse pulled the wagon down the road.

Henry blew out a frustrated breath as he stepped back to his letterpress. The type was set, but he had no ink. Why had he thought he could complete such a daunting task as printing a copy of the New Testament in a few months? Maybe he could do it if his work weren't dependent on other people. The men in the village were keeping their promise to supply him with all that he needed—including the ingredients for his ink recipe—but they weren't in a hurry like he was.

He picked up one of the two unused candles left from his trade with Hannah. He needed more candles but didn't want to go to her, not because of the note of warning someone had written him but because of the feelings stirred by the dance they'd shared.

He'd only seen her on Sundays at church over the two weeks since the dance, and they hadn't spoken. Both weeks he'd sat with his parents on the third pew and she'd sat on the back row flanked by siblings. Her family had left before he could come up with a reason to approach.

He stretched the bones in his half-hand to relieve its stiffness. Maybe this Sunday he would muster the courage to speak to Hannah. No, he had to remove all amorous thoughts of her from his mind. She needed a book printed and he needed candles. A simple exchange of goods was all there was between them and all there could ever be.

Alas, footsteps approached the doorway. He turned, expecting to see Mr. Foster. Instead, he was greeted by the scornful pout of Miss Cecelia Foster. She held up a covered jar and leveled her gaze on him. "Father said you needed soot."

Henry took the jar and matched her glower. "Thank you."

"Don't thank me. Thank my father. He scraped the chimney this morning."

"I will thank him next time I see him." He set the jar on his worktable, avoiding eye contact with the woman he'd once adored. "Thank you, all the same. Good day, Miss Foster."

Cecelia didn't leave.

He flicked a glance at her. "Was there something else?"

She crossed her thin arms tightly over her flower-printed bodice. "I see you haven't changed."

He eyed her from nose to knees and back up. "Nor have you."

Cecelia beaded her pretty eyes. "When I heard you'd been given the print shop, I thought maybe it would mature your manners, but I was wrong."

"Something you should be used to by now."

"What?"

"Being wrong."

"Arrogant fool!" She stomped a step closer. "I was heartbroken when you didn't ask to court me last year after all that pursuit, but now I'm grateful. You saved me from a lifetime of aggravation and hurt. Not that we ever would have married."

"We would if you'd had your way."

She shook her head. "No, I wouldn't have married you. I see that clearly now. And you know why?"

He didn't dignify her captious question with an answer. He'd quickly discovered he didn't want a life with Cecelia Foster and her emotional vicissitudes. He looked away but she continued unabated. "Because you are incapable of loving anyone but yourself, Henry Roberts."

At that his fingers curled into his palms, blanching his knuckles. The modicum of truth in her summation carved his heart from his chest. He wasn't capable of loving a woman enough to make a relationship worthwhile.

He too was relieved it hadn't worked out between him and Cecelia. He hadn't thought it would ever matter, that he'd ever try to love again, but now he found himself longing for Hannah more each day. He shouldn't. Eventually he would hurt her too. Cecelia was right.

He busied himself with the utensils on the worktable, not wanting to give her the satisfaction of knowing she was riling him. "I said good day, Miss Foster."

She propped her bony wrists on her hips and acerbic words slithered from her tongue. "Fine. You may dismiss me, Henry, but I will not forget what you did."

"I'm sorry my existence offends you."

"You led me on."

"I apologized."

"I deserve better."

His patience ended. "You will get nothing else from me."

She huffed and spun on her heel. He stared down at the utensils on the worktable. When he was sure she had left, he looked up. Though she played the victim, Cecelia Foster had the gumption to recover from their failed relationship. She would love again. Still, he regretted how he'd kept her affections alive even after his had fizzled. He could not do that to Hannah. She was different, vulnerable, already wrapped in grief.

It was the way she differed from other women that enchanted him. She was as passionate as the dramatic girls, but her passion usually stayed tucked beneath a shroud of loneliness. He wanted to peel it back as he had when they argued, just to see the way the fire lit her eyes. The dance they shared had proven that if he stoked the flame, she would respond.

If only they could have another quiet moment together, he could find out more about her. Maybe she was the one woman in the Land he could love. Maybe she would see past his scarred hand and find his heart worth loving. But what if, after all that, she annoyed him or found his logic insulting or made demands he couldn't meet?

He couldn't bear the guilt if she fell in love with him and his love ran out. Then again, she might surprise him; she already had many times. She might keep her wits about her. He might be the one to lose himself. She might discover who he really was and reject him. From that he might never recover, but he could no longer deny his need to find out.

CHAPTER TWELVE

Mist droplets floated into the air, making the granite slab behind the waterfall appear to move. The rock face was more stalwart than the soldiers who guarded Prince Aric's palace. Hannah toed off her shoes and lowered her satchel of freshly written pages to the ground. Adeline would love this place.

Hannah padded through the wet moss until she stood at the edge of a cool stone ledge. She crouched down and dipped one finger into the clear water that ran past her rocky perch. Maybe she should write a scene at a spring like this, just for Adeline. Every woman needed a place of solace in nature where she could be alone now and then.

The spring water that showered over the waterfall and fed this rippling pool had inspired more than the name of Hannah's village; it fueled her writing and stilled her soul. It was here by the water's edge that she'd come after her mother's burial, and here where—over the years—she'd wiped her tears and stared up at the wide blue sky above, praying for the strength to keep her promise.

Above the ten-foot drop of the fall, water burbled beneath the surface as it rushed out of the earth. The constant hum and flow of water matched the activity in her imagination. Yet in the midst of all that swirled in her mind, she found peace on these rocks and in her story. The combination of writing while being at the springs was the closest thing to Heaven she could imagine ever finding on Earth.

Sometimes during the winter months, she found shelter from the wind and mist in the rocks behind the waterfall. She studied the shadow of the shallow cave where she'd spent many chilly afternoons, sitting in its alcove, safely hidden from the elements. That seemed to be the place where she always wrote romantic prose, as if her story flourished most when she was least visible. It was difficult to get to the cave behind the waterfall without getting misted, but it was worth it. Her feet had memorized the path over the years.

No matter where she chose to write at the springs, within the hour, she had to go back to her family's house, back to her promise. Her daily routine was fixed in a perpetual state of chore and challenge while rearing her siblings, so she clung to Aric and Adeline's story as if God had given it to her to replace the freedom she'd lost when her mother died. Writing was her escape, her serenity, her expression of life and love and God's redemptive plan, but at her father's request and Olivia's suggestion, she would soon allow a stranger into her private world.

Henry Roberts wasn't really a stranger; they'd lived near each other since their families had settled in this uncharted land. But she'd kept busy at home and he'd spent his years in the print shop, so they hadn't interacted often. She had spoken to him more in the past three weeks than she had in the entire eight years they'd been neighbors. What little she'd learned about him hadn't eased her mind about him reading her story.

It wasn't that she feared he would break her trust by telling someone about her story, thereby ruining her inner retreat, but that he might judge her writing inadequate, or as he'd put it, *unworthy of ink.*

She raised her skirt and sat on the slippery rock, plunging her feet into the refreshing water flowing past. Leaning her palms behind her, she raised her face to the canopy of trees that blocked the afternoon sun. Just as its warm rays could freckle skin this time of year but thaw ice in winter, so Henry Roberts had proven to be a complex mixture of harm and help. His defensive arrogance during their quarrels had melted when they danced, showing he did possess pleasantness—though not much sentiment—beneath his impatient surface.

Their dance had sparked something not in her heart but in her imagination. She would never admit to him how he'd ignited her story, energizing it to near completion. All that was left was deciding on the ending—for she favored a happy one—then the dreaded edits and revisions.

But she didn't have to think about editing right now, or any of her responsibilities. She had half an hour before she needed to be back in the kitchen preparing her family's dinner.

The gentle flow of clear water around her feet and the breeze that rustled gray leaf trees overhead lulled her to close her eyes. Water drops pattered the rocks near the fall, and songbirds called to each other from the limbs above. As she drew in a long breath of the rich, earthy air, her shoulders relaxed. The water soothed her skin, swirling between her toes and over her ankles. The sound of it lapping at the rock beneath her cleansed her mind. As she hummed a contented sigh, the murmur of men's voices jostled her from her peace.

Her eyelids sprang open.

She scanned the waterfall to her left, the opposite edge of the pool, and the stream leaving the pool to her right, but saw no one. She drew her feet out of the water and stood, shaking out her skirt to cover her bare legs.

The voices grew louder as laughing men approached through the forest. Stretching her neck, she peered around the tall tussock grass. A blur of dark pants and light shirts moved beyond the thicket as the men grew closer on the path. Soon, their faces came into view.

Mr. Roberts, Simon, and Henry stopped short when they saw her. The ends of fishing poles wobbled overhead from their abrupt halt. Their grins faded as their amused time together was jarred by her presence. The men exchanged an uncertain glance.

Mr. Matthew Roberts touched his wide-brimmed hat in greeting. "Afternoon, Miss Vestal," the older man said, his kind smile puffing his chop-shaped side whiskers.

She slid her wet feet into her shoes, which had warmed in a shard of sunlight that broke through the canopy. "Good afternoon, Mr. Roberts. Simon. Henry."

Simon nodded politely then looked at his father, as if waiting for a cue to whether they should stay even though their destination was occupied. Henry stood a pace behind his father and brother with the top half of his face obscured by the rim of his gray felt hat and the clean-shaven bottom half stoic. The thin shadow between his lips was set in an unreadable straight line.

She eyed Henry for a moment. Why hadn't he responded when she said hello? Since the dance, she'd only seen him at church in passing. Perhaps he didn't feel friendly toward her despite what she thought was growth in their friendship. His gaze was fixed on her. He didn't nod or smile or speak.

Trying not to be offended, she lifted her satchel's strap from the ground before any more could be said. "I was just leaving." She returned Mr. Roberts's warm smile. "Enjoy your fishing, gentlemen."

Henry stepped out of his father's shadow. "Allow me to walk you home."

Both of the other men snapped their faces toward Henry. Mr. Roberts glanced between Henry and Hannah for one confused moment before understanding dawned in his eyes. He cleared his throat. "No need to leave on our account, Miss Vestal. The fishing's usually no good up here. Simon and I were headed downstream."

Henry gave his father an incredulous look, but Mr. Roberts ignored it and took Henry's pole from him. "Catch up to us when you can, son." He walked on, leading Simon along the stream.

Hannah watched their backs until they were out of sight. She half hoped they would come back so she wouldn't be left alone with Henry and half hoped Henry would ask her to dance to the music of the waterfall.

Henry stood silently rubbing his scarred palm with the thumb of the other hand, studying her. "Were you really leaving?"

"To accommodate you all."

"So I thought. We disturbed your solitude." He stepped closer. Fallen twigs and flattened grass crackled underfoot. He pointed at the forest path where it descended the slope. "From up there, you looked perfectly content. I spotted you before you heard Simon and my father's jollity. I've never seen you look so… content."

He must have spotted her sitting on the rock and dangling her feet in the water without her knowing anyone was near. Her cheeks warmed. She turned her face to the waterfall and threaded the satchel strap between her fingers. "This is my favorite place in the settlement."

"Mine too." His voice grew closer as he crossed the path to stand beside her. He took off his hat. "If I ever wanted to build a house in the Land, it would be here."

"Please don't. This place shouldn't belong to any one man."

The tree shadows covered him, making his reddish hair seem brown, but the light reflecting off the water brightened his irises to a haunting crystalline blue. The clarity of his eyes and the intensity of his gaze caught her by surprise. If she looked long enough, she might see his soul.

And she wanted to.

The thought shook her more than his captivating stare. How could she be attracted to this man who doubted he would enjoy her writing? To this man who had judged her story unworthy of ink before reading a word of it?

Try as she might, no recollection of his off-putting behavior made the awakening feelings go away. Standing there beside the water with sunlight flitting through the canopy, she forgot about her story and her responsibilities and her grief. All that existed was Henry Roberts and his unrelenting gaze.

"I wouldn't," he said at last.

"Wouldn't what?"

"Build a house here. Try to claim this land." He opened a palm toward the waterfall and broke his stare with a satisfied grin. "You're right: the springs belong to the village. No one will build a house here, not as long as my father and I are on the council. I only meant that if it were possible to live here, it would be delightful."

"Oh," she said on a thoughtless breath, still shaken by the deluge of feelings pumping out of her heart. "Delightful, indeed."

He combed his fingers through his hair, pushing it away from his face. "How is the water?"

"Perfect."

He lifted his feet one at a time and removed his shoes and socks. "Since you don't have to leave, do you mind if I join you?" he asked as he rolled his trouser cuffs up to his knees.

His sudden joviality intrigued her, and seeing as how he was preparing to hang his feet in the water rather than walk her home, she gave heed to his confidence. Part of her wanted to balk at his presumption and leave him there alone, but her feet were already out of her shoes. She returned to the edge of the gurgling pool and sat.

Henry lowered himself to the slippery rock beside her. He sighed. "It would make a lovely back yard though, wouldn't it?"

She considered what it might be like if her family's house had been built here instead of a half-mile away. "For a while, but eventually, I'd need some place to go to get away from everything. I suppose if my family lived here, I'd escape to somewhere else."

He pointed to the shadow behind the waterfall. "There is a little cave back there."

"Yes, it has sheltered me many times." Though she felt him face her, she kept her eyes forward and watched a dragonfly hover over the water's rippling surface. "I come here to write on Sunday afternoons but only if the girls are occupied and father doesn't need me at home."

He glanced at her satchel, which was on the ground behind them. "If this place is your inspiration, then I look forward to reading your story."

The kindness in his voice made her breath catch, but the weight of his words—that he would read hers— caused a ping of regret. She had to remember why she was pushing herself to finish her story and subjecting her private world to outside scrutiny. "It's all for my father. He will be so pleased if I can present him with a bound copy of the story for his birthday. My mother would have been proud too. Perhaps it's more for her."

"It's an excellent way to honor her memory."

The conversation had taken a sadder tone than she intended, but sitting beside him on the stone by the babbling water, she could say anything to him. "I honor her every day by taking care of my family. I try to, at least. Lately, I've been writing so much at night that I'm sleepwalking through my days. I've never been happier with my writing, but I feel like I'm failing at my promise."

Henry was close enough his arm brushed hers. "What promise?"

She had never told anyone about her last conversation with her mother, except David. Shortly after their mother's death, she'd found her brother crying in the barn. He was only twelve at the time, and she'd tried to comfort him by assuring him she would take care of him and all their siblings just as she'd promised Mother. David had often used that conversation against her, throwing it in her face anytime she was doing something besides cooking and cleaning.

Could she trust Henry and tell him?

She studied his profile. He was six years her senior, and would one day take his father's place as a village elder. Though stern in his logic, he'd proven tenderness when she spoke of her mother. Still, she'd never confided in a man outside her family before. She fixed her eyes on the water and let her vision blur. "When my mother was dying, she told me it was up to me as the oldest to take care of our home and my brothers and sisters. She made me promise her I would put our family first. She said to keep writing my stories but put them first."

"That's an unfair burden to put on a young woman."

"What choice did she have out here in this isolated settlement? She was dying and leaving behind six children—two of them toddlers—and I was the closest thing to a mother they had. I've raised them thus far. David and Wade don't need me much anymore—just cooking and cleaning and mending. Doris needs me in a different way now that she's thirteen. I still have years to go with the twins."

He didn't speak, and she liked his silence. The quiet togetherness suited her. After a moment, he leaned his palms on the mossy ground behind him. "Then what will you do… when they are grown?"

A surprised chuckle escaped her throat. "I'll be too old to care."

"Certainly not."

"I suppose I'll have more time to write. Although, since David will inherit my family's home and orchard, he will probably keep me cooking and cleaning all day to earn my keep."

"Unless he marries."

"Ah, yes. Then he and his happy bride will banish me to the cellar."

Henry grinned and lifted a sarcastic eyebrow. "A cellar would make a fine home."

She smiled, happily playing along. "Yes, quiet and cozy. It would be the perfect place to write."

He raised a finger as if making a point. "And since you're so good at making candles, you would have plenty of light down there."

"I suppose so." She swished her feet in the water, upsetting a turtle that was sunning itself on a nearby rock. "See, my spinsterhood won't be so bad. How about you?"

His smile grew. "Oh, I'd make a frightful spinster."

They both laughed. She nudged him, liking that he was close enough to touch. "No, I meant: what will you do now that your father has given you the print shop and Simon will take over the farm? Where will you live?"

"Perhaps Simon will offer me the cellar." He glanced at her and when she didn't laugh, his smile faded too. "I might ask Gabe to help me add a room onto the print shop. I don't need much space."

"What if you have a family someday?"

He lifted his palms from the ground and stared at the bumps on his left hand where he'd lost two fingers. "That's not something I'll ever have to worry about. I haven't had…" He kept looking at his hands and rubbed his palm, but he didn't finish his sentence.

Though she wasn't sure what he'd stopped himself from saying, she knew the feeling behind his unspoken words. "I'll never have to worry about it either."

Whatever thought had come to his mind had locked him away in some dark place. She wished she had said nothing about him someday having a family. Surely there was something she could say to lure him back to the present. Nothing came to mind. She watched him rub his scarred palm. "Does it hurt?"

"Sometimes. Not now."

"You were rubbing it like it was sore."

He drew an outline of his missing fingers. "Phantom itching. Sometimes rubbing my palm makes it stop." He folded his hands and looked out over the water. "Sometimes nothing makes it stop."

She remembered back to when he'd injured his hand while helping raise the new barn on his family's property a few years ago. Both of the Doctors Ashton had worked through the night to save as much of his hand as possible. Then the fever had set in, and everyone feared he would die of infection. "You are stronger than all of us. At one point, you weren't expected to live through the night, and then there you were, sitting in the church the next Sunday morning."

His back straightened. "It wasn't by my strength."

"Right, God healed you. Even still, I remember being amazed by your recovery."

"It was God, yes, but through the medicine He has surrounded us with."

"What do you mean?"

He turned his gaze to her. "If I am to tell you, I must swear you to secrecy."

A quick thrill tightened her belly. "Secrecy?"

He nodded, his expression more serious than she'd ever seen.

She matched his gaze. "All right. I won't tell anyone. What medicine?"

He motioned to the trees overhead. "Tea made from the gray leaf tree."

"Tea?"

"Jonah made tea for me from the gray leaf. It saved Marian's life once, but it put her in a coma, so the senior Doctor Ashton forbade Jonah ever to give it to a patient again. When Jonah knew I would die from the infection, he told me about the gray leaf tea and the potential danger." His eyes darkened. "At that point, I didn't care if I lived or died. I hoped the gray leaf would put me to sleep and I'd never awaken. But I did. Two days later. The infection was gone, and my wounds were healed."

Amazement dropped Hannah's mouth open. When Henry looked at her, she promptly closed it. "What was it like… the gray leaf medicine?"

"Blissful. It removed my pain. For a short time it made me forget I'd ever been hurt. And it sped my recovery by one hundred times."

She thought about her mother's illness. "Do you think it might have helped my mother?"

"There is no way of knowing. I'm certain Doctor Ashton did everything he could for your mother."

"I'm sure he did," she said, but still wondered.

"He truly believes the gray leaf medicine is more poison than cure. That is why he's forbidden Jonah from using it."

"What did your parents say?"

"They don't know it's what cured me. No one does other than Jonah and Marian… and now you."

Struck by the sweetness of him sharing his secret, she inched her arm over until it pressed against him. The breeze rustled the gray leaf tree limbs overhead. She looked up with a new appreciation of the remarkable tree that grew all around them but nowhere else on earth.

They sat quietly for a moment while shadows played across the water and their legs and the rocks. Without a word he scooped her hand into his and held it lightly. They both watched their joined hands. He let out a long breath, and when he spoke his voice was barely louder than the water that flowed by. "Hannah, I've thought about you every moment since the dance."

Despite the warmth in the air, all the muscles in her body froze. He hadn't stopped thinking about her in nearly two weeks? Was he in love with her? She too had felt something between them that night under the oval moon and even now sitting together by the stream with their feet dangling in the water. But was it love?

All at once the emerging feelings in her heart gurgled to the surface like the springs bubbling nearby. Henry Roberts hadn't simply inspired her to write, he'd awakened her heart. Was that what had fueled her writing these past few days? Her attraction to Henry Roberts?

She opened her mouth to respond to him, but her words dissolved on her tongue.

Disappointment flashed across his face. He loosened his hold. "I'm sorry."

He began to pull away, so she entwined her fingers with his to stop him. "Don't."

"Don't what?"

"Don't apologize. Don't go."

He gave her hand a squeeze. "I won't." He looked at her with both hope and regret in his eyes. "Until you tell me to."

His gaze moved to her lips, just as it had at the end of their dance, but this time he leaned in and kissed her. A nervous quiver fluttered her insides as he pressed his lips to hers. Unsure of what to do, she closed her eyes, but before she could absorb his kiss, men's voices rumbled in the distance downstream. She quickly pulled away.

Feeling caught in mischief, she scampered to her wet feet and peered around the thicket. Mr. Roberts and Simon were traipsing up the path along the stream. She slipped back into her shoes and pretended to watch the waterfall while Henry casually dried his feet and tugged on his boots.

"Oh, you're still here," Mr. Roberts said as they rounded the bushes. He glanced from her to Henry and back again. "Sorry to interrupt. Turns out the fish aren't biting downstream."

Hannah forced a smile though she was certain her cheeks were cardinal red and Mr. Roberts knew she'd just been kissed. She hugged her satchel to her chest. "I really should be on my way home."

Henry unrolled his trouser cuffs and sent his father a dour look. "I'll walk her home."

"No, thank you," she said more insistently than she'd intended. "I should go alone."

Henry caught her eye, and her forced smile melted. For an instant it was only the two of them again. His expression changed slightly, but the connection was undeniable. He took one step forward then stopped, his air of formality returning. "Very well. Good day, Miss Vestal."

CHAPTER THIRTEEN

Henry stabbed a chunk of venison with his fork and glowered at Simon. He wanted to lunge across the dinner table and rip the smirk off his brother's face. Instead, he chewed his dinner, grinding the seasoned meat until his jaw ached.

Simon chuckled like a ninny as he told their mother and siblings about Henry and Hannah at the springs. "We gave Henry plenty of time to walk Hannah home, but when we came back upstream, there they were, soaking their feet in the water, sitting close like a couple of lovebirds." Bits of potato stuck to Simon's fat lower lip. "You should have seen Henry's face when we caught him."

"Caught nothing," Henry mumbled. Thank heavens Simon hadn't seen them kiss. He would have gotten an even bigger laugh at that. And Henry wouldn't have been able to restrain his anger so well.

For a time Henry had thought it was Simon who left the note at the print shop telling him to stay away from Hannah, but if Simon were in love with her, he wouldn't be having this much fun mocking them.

"A couple of lovebirds," Simon repeated himself, laughing.

Ellenore's eyes were rounded happily, but she wasn't laughing with Simon. "Are you courting her then?" she asked Henry with a hopeful tone in her voice.

He would answer his favorite sister's questions later, but not now, not in front of the whole family with Simon's battle-ax of mockery in full swing.

He gave Ellenore a look, hoping she understood. Ellenore sent a smile across the table to Hazel, who passed the happy expression to their mother. The three younger children were oblivious to the meaning of the glances.

Priscilla lifted a ceramic bowl of cheesy potatoes and offered it to Simon. "Here, son. Finish these off while your father tells us about the… village business."

With Simon's attention on his food, Priscilla nodded at Matthew. He took his cue and told the family about the elder's latest plans.

Henry wasn't listening. His mind drifted back to the springs and to Hannah. It was illogical for a man of his intellect and satisfaction in bachelorhood to be preoccupied with a woman, but he'd thought of nothing else all afternoon. Sitting beside her on the rock, he'd been close enough to hear the change in her breath when he touched her, close enough to count the golden specks in the brown of her eyes, close enough to know she wanted to be kissed.

And how he'd wanted to kiss her too.

He hadn't planned it, but when he saw her by the springs, he had to know if she felt the same way about him. Now it was clear. Yet, the more his affection for her grew, the more his thoughts clouded.

With one simple kiss he'd complicated their relationship. Did this mean they would court? If so, he should do the honorable thing and speak to her father first. It seemed too soon for that. He'd become attracted to Hannah, kissed her, couldn't stop thinking about her, wanted to pummel his brother for mocking them, but did any of it mean he should change his life and plan for marriage?

He'd never felt like this when he wanted to court Peggy Cotter, or even with Cecelia Foster. For some enigmatic reason everything was different with Hannah. Hannah was different. So much thought and passion churned beneath her surface, and he ached to investigate. That investigation would require courting. But there was more to courting than spending time together. The elders had made it clear that in the village of Good Springs, the purpose of courting was to determine if the couple was well suited for marriage. *We are too small a population to toy with each other's affections*, Reverend Colburn always said.

So he hadn't asked Cecelia to court and look how that turned out.

He shouldn't move forward blindly and risk hurting Hannah or himself. But did he want marriage? Was he capable of loving Hannah how she deserved to be loved?

At some point, Matthew stopped telling the family about the mundane village business. He sopped up the last drips of gravy on his plate with a heel of bread then ate it. After everyone finished dinner, the youngest girls cleared the table.

While the women chatted and washed dishes, Henry needed to be alone and think. He stood from the table and looked at Priscilla. "Thank you for dinner, Mother."

She tilted her head a degree the way mothers did when they knew something was wrong. Without giving her a chance to ask, he climbed the narrow staircase to the bedroom he shared with Simon to get his satchel before he went back to the print shop. Pausing in the corner of the room, he knelt to pull a wooden box from under his bedstead. After a check of the doorway, he opened the box.

Beneath a stack of nature sketches, he found the portrait he'd drawn after Mrs. Susanna Vestal's funeral six years ago. Mrs. Vestal's appearance had changed rapidly in the months before her death, but this portrait was how he remembered her. Face full of life, noble cheekbones, and light in her golden brown eyes. She'd babysat him when he was a young boy back in Virginia, and he'd enjoyed the way she told all the children stories to amuse them. He would never forget her ability to make up the stories as she told them.

Hannah had inherited more than her mother's features. She possessed her mother's creativity and gentle spirit. He'd soon find out about her storytelling skills. For both of their sakes, he hoped her story was worth printing.

The more he thought of Hannah, the more he wanted to be with her. It was both noble and a pity she had committed her life to raising her siblings. *I still have years to go with the twins*, she'd said.

Henry lowered the sketch and stared at the wall. What was he doing by interfering with the Vestal family? They needed Hannah. He was allowing his attraction to her to drive his thoughts.

"She looks just like her mother, doesn't she?" Priscilla said from the doorway.

Henry laid the sketch back in the wooden box and slid it under the bed. "She does."

"Have you shown Hannah that sketch?"

"No."

Priscilla stepped into the room. "You should. She might like to see it."

Though his mother meant well, he didn't want her telling him what he should and shouldn't do with Hannah. He slid the sketch into his satchel as he rounded the bedstead. "I need to go back to work."

Priscilla sat on the edge of his bed and smoothed the pleats in her skirt. "Hannah's a special girl," she said, trying to lure him into a conversation he didn't want.

"Yes, she is."

"She has worked diligently to take care of her family. It takes a special kind of faithfulness to raise children that aren't your own. She is strong but delicate too."

He stepped toward the doorway. "Indeed."

"Take care that you don't hurt her, son."

He stopped and turned on the ball of his foot. "I have no intention of hurting her."

Priscilla lifted an innocent hand. "No one ever does. These things begin sweetly, but someone always gets hurt."

Someone always got hurt when he was involved. She didn't say that part, but that's what she meant. And it was always the girl who got hurt. Women took offense so easily, but he didn't want to talk about it. If any person besides his mother had brought up his flawed past, he would have harangued them with cunning wit until they regretted it.

But it was his mother, and she was right.

He took a slow breath and tried to relax his aching hand. He didn't want to hurt Hannah. By kissing her he'd moved their relationship into dangerous new territory. He couldn't forget what had happened or ignore his growing desire to be with her, but neither of them had circumstances that suited courting. He was busy with the press and didn't have the time to build a house and feed a family. She couldn't leave her responsibilities, and he would not ask her to.

"I care for Hannah a great deal." He looked away so his mother wouldn't see the doubt in his eyes. "And I won't hurt her." As the words left his mouth, he left the room.

CHAPTER FOURTEEN

Hannah walked into the church behind her father, brothers, and the twins. Though not yet nine o'clock in the morning, the warm air had thickened with humidity overnight. Heavy rain was coming. It couldn't dampen her enthusiasm for her nearly completed story or for the chance to see Henry.

The Roberts family hadn't arrived yet, but the church was nearly full. Half of Hannah's siblings dispersed inside the chapel. Doris skipped toward the front of the room and sat beside her friends. David slid into a seat two rows behind the pew their father chose. Wade craned his neck, also looking for someone, anyone, to sit with other than his sisters.

Gone were the days of the family sitting together on one pew. Such was the case with most families in Good Springs. With many of the young people growing up, marrying, and starting their own families, the weekly church services had become more about the community as a whole than one's own family.

Christopher had given the older Vestal children permission to sit where they pleased, but Hannah wouldn't leave her father and the young twins. They might feel rejected if she did. Of course, David, Wade, and Doris weren't rejecting the rest of the family by sitting elsewhere but enlarging their social spheres. It was natural, expected even. They all still mattered to each other, yet one day someone else would matter more to them.

Hannah never thought she'd want to spend her Sunday mornings anywhere other than beside her family, but after Henry's kiss, everything felt different. She'd thought of him while she brushed her hair, while she'd laced her Sunday shoes, and even now as she sat and straightened her posture. Despite a heart swelling with new feelings, she fought the urge to look for him.

She checked the twins, studied her cuticles, and flipped open the cover of her Bible, but soon her eyes searched the crowd pouring into the chapel.

Henry had yet to arrive. It shouldn't matter to her. Her family was her priority. The twins might need her during the service. She belonged here beside them. Still, it would be nice to have freedom like the other young adults. If she couldn't have a romance in real life, she could experience one in her story.

As the villagers found their seats, Hannah's mind drifted. She'd stopped berating herself for not paying attention to sermons long ago. The mind went where it willed, and she was too close to finishing her story to care.

Adeline had convinced Prince Aric to fight the atrocities of the slave traders. With swords and horses, he'd gallantly led the king's army out to fight. While he was gone, Adeline was taken prisoner by a neighboring kingdom, which she discovered had funded the kidnapping slave traders who'd stolen her from her homeland.

During Hannah's writing time last night, she had left Adeline in a dark, damp dungeon, praying Prince Aric would receive word that his beloved needed help. All that was left to write was Aric's daring rescue, defeat of the enemy, and declaration of eternal love for Adeline.

Hannah almost released a sigh, but her attention snapped back to the present.

As the chapel doors closed, Henry slipped into Hannah's row and sat beside her. He grinned. "Good morning."

"Good morning." The words fell out of her open mouth as ineloquently as a horse sipping tea. Her face warmed.

Henry didn't seem to notice her blush. He leaned in front of her and the twins to shake Christopher's hand. "Good morning, sir."

"Henry," Christopher replied. He gave Hannah a quick questioning glance then turned his gaze to the front of the room.

Reverend Colburn stepped to the lectern and began the service with prayer, beseeching God for the congregation's health, protection, unity, and provision. He thanked the Lord for the coming rain, and as if God replied, drops tinkled against the glass windowpanes and on the roof. The slow patter quickly turned into a steady downpour. When the reverend said *amen*, he raised his voice to compete with the sound.

Hannah opened her Bible along with everyone else to the passage the reverend was expounding and tried to calm her thumping heart. No man had ever shown interest in her like this before, and certainly not in public. Was everyone behind them watching them?

She held her Bible in front of Ida and Minnie so they could read along. Neither of the twins had her own copy of the Scriptures yet. Perhaps one day Henry would print Bibles for every boy and girl in the settlement. Maybe he would print many books for the children. What were his plans for the future?

Hannah glanced at him. He had his open Bible splayed in his hand and was looking at the reverend. Just when she thought her gaze had gone unnoticed, Henry shifted in his seat and slid his arm over the pew back behind her.

Now everyone behind them would be watching them.

She fixed her eyes on the page, praying the twins wouldn't notice Henry's arm. Or David. He was sitting two rows back. If he noticed, she'd never hear the end of it.

Why did it matter what David thought? She was a grown woman, and a man who liked her had awakened her heart. Did he love her? He might. Or he might be a scoundrel, a thief of affection here to rob her peace. Or he might one day be her husband.

What a silly waste of energy! She could no sooner get married and leave her family than she could sprout wings and fly to the fictional land in her book. They needed her to keep her promise, and her characters needed her to finish her story. Henry Roberts might be interested in her, but he didn't *need* her. Not like her family did.

She tried to remind herself of her first encounters with Henry. He was aloof and independent. So what if he'd said he hadn't stopped thinking about her since the dance? Good Springs was a small, isolated village with little entertainment. His attraction was probably nothing more than a passing fancy, and she'd be a fool to make more of it.

Still, all she could think of was the warmth radiating from his body and the minty scent of his breath.

He might not be thinking of her at all. He was probably thinking about his work. She should think about hers too if she wasn't going to listen to the sermon. She tried to recall the scene in her story she wanted to write later, but her stubborn thoughts were fixed on the man beside her. He'd kissed her, sweetly, privately, but now was publicly showcasing his affection by draping his arm across the seat behind her.

Or was he?

Maybe he always rested in such a position when he sat casually in a crowd. Many of the men did. It was a relaxed posture, the very reason some elders had objected to the pews having backs. When any other man sat with his arm behind his sweetheart, she judged it a possessive posture, as if he were staking his claim. But maybe Henry was just at ease in her company.

That was a much more tolerable thought. He was simply enjoying her company, becoming her friend. Yes, a friendly gesture—that was all. A friend wouldn't make demands of her life that she couldn't oblige.

Reverend Colburn referenced another scripture passage, and Henry took his arm down to flip through his Bible. He held the book with both hands and looked at the reverend for the rest of the sermon, save for the occasional glance at Hannah. She wished he'd put his arm behind her again.

After the service, Henry made small talk with Christopher then complimented the twins on their curls. "Pretty like your big sister," he said.

Minnie pushed in front of Ida. "But my hair is prettier isn't it?"

"No, my curls are bouncier!" Ida protested.

"There now girls." Christopher put a fatherly hand on each of the twins, ushering them toward the door. "Say thank you and good day to Mr. Roberts." He looked up at Henry. "Come to our house for dinner tonight."

"Thank you, sir, but it's my sister's birthday."

"Perhaps another time, then."

Hannah silently watched the exchange, her stomach flipping like a fish in a frying pan. Why was her father inviting Henry to dinner? Did he know they had kissed? Had Henry spoken to her father about her?

Rain poured from the sky as the family stepped out of the chapel. Christopher opened the family's big umbrella and passed it to Hannah. The twins gathered closely beside her while she held it overhead. Doris popped open a new umbrella, one made by Mrs. Owens with a gray leaf wood frame and waxed cotton fabric. Christopher and David slapped on their wide-brimmed hats to shield themselves from the downpour, but Wade joined Doris under her umbrella.

Doris let Wade hold the umbrella's curved handle. As soon as they were down the chapel steps, Doris's voice fought the rain for volume. "I'll say, Hannah, that was a delightful surprise seeing Henry Roberts sit by you. Aren't you intrigued with him? You should let him court you."

Hannah watched the road ahead, trying to guide the twins around the deepest of the puddles. "Not now, Doris."

"You would make a handsome couple. He is dashing, don't you think?"

David flipped up his collar to shield his neck from the rain. "Shut it, Doris."

Their father's voice came from behind them. "Speak kindly to your sister."

"Fine," David huffed. "Shut it, please."

Unabated by her brother's scolding, Doris continued. "I think Hannah is the luckiest lady in the village. If a man came to sit by me and put his arm around me like that, all of my friends would die of jealousy."

Christopher said, "It is never charitable to want others to be jealous, Kitten."

Doris added a twinge of whininess to her voice. "I meant it as a compliment, Father. Hannah finally has a suitor, and for it to be someone as dapper as Henry, she should be glowing."

David raised his voice. "He isn't her suitor!"

"What's a suitor?" Minnie asked.

Hannah wanted to cover the twins' ears, but her hands were busy keeping the umbrella steady in the rain. She ground her teeth together. "Please drop the subject, everyone."

She hadn't figured out what Henry was to her or what he wanted to be or what she was to him because none of it mattered—at least not now and maybe not for years to come. Aric and Adeline's romance was the only love story she should be concerned with at the moment.

Once home, the family hung their dripping overcoats in the mudroom. Hannah sent Doris upstairs to help the twins change while she got lunch on the table. Christopher and the boys returned to the kitchen first, talking about the growing puppies and what homes they would go to once they were weaned.

Doris stepped into the kitchen during their discussion. "I think Henry should have one of the puppies."

"Doris!" Hannah warned.

"Well, Sarah Ashton told me Henry is trying to make the printing press a village-supported trade, so I think we should at least offer him a puppy."

David narrowed his eyes at Doris. "He's not getting one of my dogs."

Christopher lifted a palm, silencing them both. "Kitten, this is none of your concern. David, you and Henry will be on the elder council together your whole lives. You should respect him."

David dropped into his seat at the table looking more like a sulky adolescent than the eighteen-year-old that he was. "He's no good for Hannah."

"David!" Hannah's hand slipped as she carried a tray of cheese to the table. The tray clattered on the table, drawing everyone's attention.

Doris jumped to her aid. "Now you've upset Hannah. What have you got against Henry?"

David crossed his arms over his chest. "I don't like him."

"You don't have to like him," Christopher said, "but you do have to respect him and your sister. Hannah is an adult and can make her own decisions."

After Hannah slowly lowered herself into her seat at the table, Christopher said the blessing. She didn't speak for the rest of the meal.

Once the table was cleared and the dishes washed, she went to the window in the mudroom to check the sky.

Christopher shuffled into the kitchen from the parlor. "Has it stopped?"

"For now." Hannah picked up the plate of scraps for the dogs. "The wind has died off. I need out of the house for a while."

Christopher nodded and took a step away, then turned back and grinned slightly. "Just so you know... I like him."

"Who?"

"Henry. He's a good man. Hard worker."

"Father, I don't want to talk about Henry."

He raised a palm in surrender. "Well, if you do—"

"I don't." She balanced the plate of scraps on one hand and turned the doorknob with the other. "I'll be back in time to start dinner."

The break in the clouds and the lack of voices outside made her wish she'd brought her writing paper. If the rain was over, she could go to the springs and write. As she walked into the barn, she glanced back at the house. If she went back for her satchel, the girls might ask to go with her. She needed time alone more than anything. She hadn't been able to think through her story during church, so she could use the time to plan her final scene.

After giving the table scraps to the dogs, she stopped in front of Zelda's stall and fed her a carrot. The wind whipped past the barn, slamming the door shut. Hannah petted the horse. "Don't worry, girl, the storm is over. I have one quiet hour before I have to be back in the kitchen, and I will spend it well." She reached for a bridle that hung on the wall. "Let's go for a ride."

CHAPTER FIFTEEN

Henry sat at the far end of the table in his family's kitchen while his mother and Ellenore washed the dishes from Hazel's birthday dinner. The air in the room was thick with merriment and the scent of roasted chicken. Matthew Roberts had spent the better part of the meal steering every conversation to the subject of holy matrimony, eyeing Hazel and her suitor, Arnold McIntosh, all the while. The three youngest children had gone into the parlor to play after dinner, but everyone else stayed in the kitchen, knowing what their father and Arnold had planned.

Rain pounded the windows as Matthew nudged Arnold. "Go on, boy. Haven't you something to say to my daughter?"

Hazel blushed and glanced at Henry nervously. Henry nodded once to assure his sister the coming surprise from her suitor was a pleasant one.

Ellenore wiped her hands on a dishtowel and walked toward the table. Simon hovered behind Henry's chair, picking his teeth. Outside, the driving rain pattered against the house, but inside the room fell silent, save for Arnold as he knelt before Hazel and professed his love.

Henry leaned forward. There was something satisfying about watching a young man fidget and sweat as he asked a woman to marry him. Arnold's fearful expression relaxed as he spoke of his devotion to Hazel and his dreams for their future together. She tearfully accepted his proposal.

Joyous applause filled the cozy kitchen. The children ran in from the parlor, asking what was happening. A twinge of jealousy pinged inside Henry as the happy couple embraced. He was the eldest; he should have been the first to get married.

Henry left the table and paced to the window. Though still light outside, heavy rain obstructed the view to the road. A white line of melting hailstones lined the garden. Thunder rumbled all around.

Ellenore came beside him. "Hazel might be the first of us to the altar, but she isn't the only one in love."

Henry broke his gaze from the storm-tossed yard and lifted an eyebrow at his favorite sister. "Have you got a sweetheart now, Elle?"

Smiling, she popped him on the shoulder with the back of her hand. "Not me. You."

Hannah wasn't his sweetheart. Not yet. No matter how much he'd tried to resist pursuing her, when he saw her at church this morning, he couldn't stay away. His heart was dragging him irrationally forward into a relationship he wasn't capable of sustaining.

If the past was any indicator, he was in dangerous territory. He didn't have to tell Ellenore. She'd witnessed every one of his failed relationships. First having to leave Lilly in Virginia, then his infatuation with Peggy Cotter, and more recently, his inability to please Cecelia Foster. With each attempt at love—and each failure—his heart sank deeper within him. He couldn't describe what was happening now between him and Hannah, so he certainly wouldn't talk about it. He lowered his chin and gave Ellenore a look to stop the conversation before it began.

Matthew raised his cup and clinked it with a salt spoon, commanding everyone's attention. "Here, here! Gather 'round, family." His voice filled with fatherly pride. "Arnold beseeched me some time ago for Hazel's hand, and I heartily gave him my blessing. My dearest Hazel, you have been everything a daughter should be. You deserve a lifetime of happiness. I have no doubt Arnold will make you a fine husband."

A fine husband—something Henry never would be.

A frantic knock rattled the front door, ending Matthew's toast. The children ran to the door as Priscilla opened it.

Wade Vestal stepped inside with his young face red and rainwater dripping from his cap. "Is Hannah here?" he asked, panting.

Priscilla answered, "No, she isn't."

Wade's voice broke. "She left the house this afternoon and hasn't come back."

Priscilla drew her head back. "That's not like Hannah."

"We searched our property but couldn't find her. Father thought she might have come here."

Henry's heart surged into his throat. He crossed the kitchen floor in three quick strides and parted his siblings. "When did you see her last?"

"After lunch. She went outside when the rain let up." Wade flashed Henry a sour glance and quickly returned his gaze to Priscilla. "She took our lunch scraps to the dogs in the barn. We thought she stayed out there to do chores, but she didn't come back when it started storming."

Henry's sisters were crowding into the doorway and Simon too.

From across the room Matthew asked, "What's happened?"

Priscilla shooed the children away from the door and guided Wade farther inside. "It seems Hannah Vestal is missing."

"Missing?" Matthew's eye widened. "In this weather?"

The mumbles and questions rose around Henry. He swatted the air to silence them and stepped closer to Wade. "Did she take anything with her?"

Wade inched away from Henry. "No, but Zelda is gone too."

Matthew joined them near the door. "She probably rode to Olivia and Gabe's house. I sometimes see her ride Zelda past on Sunday afternoons."

When Henry had talked to Hannah at the springs last week, she had said it was her favorite place in the Land. She probably went there to write during the break in the storm. "Did you check the springs?"

Wade shook his head. "She always tells our father when she's going to the springs. She only said that she was going outside. Father thought she meant to the barn. Since we can't find her, he thought maybe she went to someone's house."

Matthew slid his arms into his overcoat. "You check the springs, son. I will ride out to Gabriel's."

Henry nodded in agreement with his father's plan.

Simon patted Henry's back. "I'll come with you."

Matthew paused at the door and glanced between Henry and Simon. "We will find her faster if we spread out. Simon, walk over to the Cotters' house and ask if they have seen her."

Simon looked at Henry as if confirming the order. "I'll do whatever you need me to do."

"Thank you," Henry answered, grateful to have his brother's support, "but Father is right. Go to the Cotters'. I'll check the springs."

Henry tried not to picture Hannah injured or trapped in floodwaters or beaten by the hail. The gut-wrenching force of fear would have crumbled him if it wasn't for his determination to find her. He pulled on his boots and slapped on his hat.

His father hurried to the barn to saddle a horse, and Simon ran toward the Cotters' farm. Henry buttoned his overcoat while dashing across the yard in the rain. Though lightning cracked in the eastern sky, he kept his eyes on the muddy path to the springs.

Why had she gone out in this weather? Break in the storm or no, she shouldn't have ventured far from the house. Even if she wanted time alone to write, she should have had more sense. What if she'd fallen into the water and drowned?

His heart ached like he'd been punched in the chest. Worrying was senseless. Illogical. She was fine, probably hiding in the cave behind the waterfall, lost in her story world and not caring about the hail and thunder that had pummeled the land. When he found her, he would scold her and escort her home and that would be the end of whatever was between them. It had to be. It would hurt, but it was better than loving her more and losing her.

That was the answer then. He couldn't love her. Not like this. Caring hurt too much.

He had work to do and a library to fill. He didn't have time to run through the rain to find missing neighbor girls.

He cut across the Vestals' property and took their well-stomped path to the springs. Beyond the orchard and pastures, the earth rose in a hill. The rain let up as he climbed the incline. Mud slurped beneath his boots, making each step more difficult. The wooded area near the springs was in sight.

He stopped to catch his breath. Something moved beyond a thicket. He squinted into the blowing mist. "Hannah?"

There was no answer.

He left the path and traipsed through the soggy grass toward the brush. A horse stood under the shelter of a tall gray leaf tree. Its reins were hooked on a low-hanging branch. The wet horse flinched, unsure if it wanted Henry's help. Its brown and white mane parted, revealing nervous black eyes.

Henry held out a hand. "Whoa there, Zelda. You're all right, girl. Where is Hannah?" He reached for the reins. The rope hadn't been tied. Hannah had left her horse in a hurry. He checked the brush, the grass, and the limbs for clues. The ground was littered with pockets of melting hailstones. Thin, water-filled boot prints dotted the mud. If the hailstorm had surprised Hannah, she would have run for cover. He didn't need to follow the prints to know where she had gone. He patted the horse. "I will be back for you as soon as I find her."

Though the rain stopped, the clouds were still thick, suffocating the last light of day. Henry deeply bent his knees for balance as he descended the slope and hurried to the water's edge. The roar of the nearby waterfall gushed violently.

The rocks where he'd sat with Hannah only a week ago were now buried under several feet of floodwater. He scanned the swelling stream as he hiked toward the cave behind the waterfall. The pool had broken free of its bank and—though it was getting too dark to see—water would be filling the shallow cave.

"Hannah?" he yelled over the tumult of rushing water. "Hannah?"

"Help!" A distant voice replied. "I'm back here!"

His boots slogged through the water as he rushed along the side of the overflowing stream. In the cave behind the falling water, the blur of a pale blue dress stood out in the fading light.

Hannah waved her arms and yelled over the sound of pouring water. "Help me!"

Henry's boots filled with water as he moved as close as possible to the rock face without falling in and being swept into the current.

Hannah stood at the cave's entrance, ankle deep in rising water. Her fawn-like eyes protruded with panic. "The water is rising quickly. I'm trapped!"

She was closer to the opposite bank than she was to him. If he could get to her, he could guide her to the far bank.

The rocks along the recessed back wall of the waterfall made a path to the cave during good weather, but the rising water and lack of light made it impossible to see where to step. If he slipped and fell into the rush of the falling water, it would take all his strength to fight the current. He yanked off his boots and overcoat and cuffed his trousers. "Stay there," he yelled to her. "I'm coming to you!"

Turning his back to the rock wall, he inched his palms along its slimy surface and toed the stones beneath the water, taking slow careful steps until he was directly behind the waterfall. Heavy spray covered his face and the fall's roar filled his ears. He turned his face in Hannah's direction. "I'm almost there!"

His left foot found the next stone and as he brought his right foot to meet it, the rock wobbled beneath him. He sucked in air, expecting to plunge into the water, but was able to regain his balance. His water-soaked socks and trouser cuffs weighted his legs. He held his breath and felt for the next rock but instead of a slab of stone, the loose pebbles of the cave entrance shifted under his feet.

Hannah gripped his forearm and pulled him toward her with one hand while holding up her dress with the other. Water lapped at her shins. "Thank God you came! How did you find me?"

"Never mind that. It's flooding fast. I have to get you out of here." He glanced back at the path he'd taken. It was now too dark to see more than a few yards away. If they fell in, she would drown. Over her head he could see the bank nearby. "We can't return to the path, but we can make it to the other side."

"I can't swim."

He held her shoulders and looked her in the eyes. "We have to get out of here before the water rises any higher."

"I'm scared."

"I know."

"What if I fall in?"

"I'm with you."

"What if I drown?"

"What if you don't?"

Something warmed her eyes, replacing the panic with trust. She nodded briskly. "All right. What should I do?"

"Watch where I step and follow me." He took her by the hand, her confidence in him bolstering his own, and led her across the water-covered boulder tops to the bank. His scarred hand throbbed as he felt along the craggy rock face, but the feel of her clinging to his good hand erased any mental complaint.

He moved slowly, checking his footing with each step as he led her from one rock to the next. With each forward movement, her quick inhales made him glance back. When his feet left the last boulder and sank into the bank's soggy ground, he let go of the rock face and offered her both hands. She took them and stepped forward, breathing heavily.

Once on solid ground, she let go of him and bent down, propping her hands on her knees. "How will we get home from here?" She panted, trying to catch her breath. "The stream is flowing too fast to cross. We can't see in the dark to hike up past the springs and cut our way through the forest to go around the water."

He unrolled his trousers and water fell from the cuffs. His wet socks clung to his feet like ink on paper. Her boots would be filled with water too. He needed to find them higher ground. He peered through the darkness at the bank, the grass beyond it, and what he could see of the tree line. How would he get her home? He couldn't think over the sound of the waterfall. "Let's follow the tree line and go farther downstream."

She walked with him until they reached the trees then stopped. He reached out, but she didn't take his hand. She covered her face and moaned. "What have I done? My family. They need me."

"They are fine. It's you everyone is worried about."

"I promised I would always be there for them, yet I was gone all afternoon. Now it's late and I didn't make them dinner and I won't be home to help the twins get ready for bed. I've never missed their bedtime, not once in their lives." Her voice came out like the whimper of a helpless creature. "I broke my promise."

"Because they had to make their own dinner?"

"Because I wasn't there with them. I just wanted an hour alone to think about my story—"

"Your story?"

"Yes. I thought the storm was over, but Zelda got spooked when the hail started. I ran to the cave for shelter and then, well, you saw." She pushed her hands through her disheveled hair and began pulling out the pins that had failed to hold it back in its usual bun. "Poor Zelda. I tossed the reins over a limb. She's probably hurt."

"Hannah, the horse is fine. She is right where you left her."

"And my family? Did you see them?"

"Only Wade. Your father sent him to our house. He thought you might have gone there."

She covered her mouth with one thin hand. "Oh, no. Your whole family knows about this? Who else?"

"My father and Simon went to search the village so probably everyone by now."

"Oh, this is horrible. I've never been so embarrassed in my life." She made a face as if disgusted with herself. "Last night I wrote a rescue scene in my story. I thought it would be a romantic experience, but this isn't romantic. It's humiliating. I shouldn't have come out here. Or I should have told my father where I was going. I should have thought of someone besides myself."

She should be glad she was alive instead of berating herself. Her emotional outburst made little sense. He waited for the annoyance to make him dislike her, but instead he shushed her gently and pulled her into his arms, not caring they were both wet and dirty. "Everything will be fine. I'll get you home. Your family will be relieved. They will want to hear about your adventure. Just think of it as another story to tell."

She slumped a little. Was she leaning into him or more embarrassed by what he'd said? He drew his head back and looked down at her. "What is it?"

"David will use this to try to ruin us."

"Us?"

"That's part of why I came out here. He was angry that you sat by me in church this morning and wouldn't stop fussing about it at lunch. I had to get away."

"He doesn't like me, does he?"

"I think he's afraid you will—"

"I will not…" He almost said *hurt you* but stopped himself. The truth was he might hurt her. He probably would. Eventually. "I'm not… without complications myself." She started to pull away, but he held her for another heartbeat. "But when I thought I might lose you tonight, I knew whatever is between us is too important to ignore."

She lifted her regal chin and the moonlight peeking between the parting clouds hit her face. She looked like war-battered nobility refusing to concede. "I won't let David interfere, even though I know why he's behaving the way he is. He lost Mother and now he's afraid of losing me."

"What about you?"

"Me?"

"Yes, you." He stroked her arms. "What do you want?"

"I don't want to lose anyone I care about again either."

It wasn't the answer he was looking for. Emotion had clouded his mind. He probably wasn't speaking logically. He needed to ask her outright if he could court her. Before he could say more, a tiny yellow light appeared across the flooded stream. He cupped his hands around his mouth and yelled, "Over here!"

The lantern light grew, and his brother called from the opposite bank. "Henry?"

"Across the water, Simon."

"Have you found Hannah?"

"She's with me."

"I saw her horse. Is she all right?"

"She's fine. We can't cross the stream. We'll have to go around through the woods, but we can't see to attempt it now."

"Stay where you are," Simon yelled to them. "I'll get help. We'll go up around the springs."

"My boots are on the ground over there near the path."

A few seconds later Simon replied, "I found them."

"Bring them to me when you come."

"Hang tight, brother. I'll get some of the men and we will be back shortly."

CHAPTER SIXTEEN

Hannah propped the back door open with a wedge of wood then walked through the mudroom and kitchen into the parlor to do the same with the front door. Though still a week until the summer solstice, the midday sun was already heating the house.

When she was a young girl and the elders were planning the voyage to the southern hemisphere, she'd imagined her new homeland having monkeys and jungle plants. They never knew the precise location where the *Providence* had run aground, but the Land enjoyed four seasons, so it was far from the tropics.

Summer had always been her favorite, and she looked forward to it the way she'd looked forward to Christmas as a child. This year, however, had been a blur. The pace of her writing during the spring had kept her from noticing the warming air and blossoming flowers. Now, spring was slipping into summer. The first storm of the season had left the air muggy, the orchard flooded, and her pride in tatters.

She tried not to think about yesterday's humiliation. Trying didn't help.

Washday puddles dotted the kitchen floor. She tiptoed between the puddles and found a scrub brush on the mudroom shelf. She tossed it to the wet floor then carried a bucket out to the well to fill.

At least her family seemed to be over last night's chaos. Warm, clear days suited them by allowing everyone to stay busy out-of-doors. David and Wade were working with their father in the barn. Doris was at the coop teaching Minnie and Ida to gather eggs.

When Hannah returned to the kitchen, the breeze blowing through the house cooled the room. She placed a folded towel under her knees and began scrubbing the hard wood. Most of the dried mud on the floor had dripped off her dress when she'd finally made it home last night. The mud had seeped into the floorboard cracks and patched them just as Henry's care for her momentarily made her feel better about her embarrassing blunder. What kind of careless ninny goes into a cave behind a waterfall for shelter during a storm?

A full day of hard work would be her penance for yesterday's failure.

As she scrubbed the mud away, David climbed the porch steps. He leaned his dirty hand against the doorjamb. "Did he touch you?"

She stayed on her hands and knees but glanced up at him. "Who?"

"You know who. Henry."

David was being a protective brother, but her relationship with Henry was none of his concern. His question rankled. She blew a wisp of hair out of her face. "Not inappropriately."

He stepped into the mudroom and pointed at the drying washboard. "Is your dress ruined?"

"I can still wear it for chores. It's only stained."

"As your reputation will be if you spend any more time alone with Henry Roberts."

"Keep your hateful opinions to yourself and get back to work, please."

He crossed his freckled arms. "The girls were terrified when you were missing."

"They're fine now."

"Did you go to the springs to see him?"

"No. Henry was with his family. Ask Wade. Henry found me and saved me from the floodwater. You should be grateful for him."

"He was the reason you ran off."

"I didn't run off." She tossed the scrub brush into the bucket. "If you're so concerned about me, why didn't you know where to look? I'm allowed to have a few moments to myself. Yes, I chose the wrong time to go out yesterday, but Henry knew where I would be because he listens to me."

"He probably listened to Cecelia Foster too until she fell for him, then he broke her heart."

Hannah swirled the scrub brush in the bucket. The dissolving mud clouded the water. She imagined chucking the whole thing at David. "This is none of your business."

"It is when my sister goes missing and upsets the family then comes home hours later with a muddy dress and a grinning suitor."

"He is not my suitor." She shot to her feet. "Get out!"

He stabbed the air with his calloused finger. "You made a promise to Mother."

Tears welled up, blurring her vision. "I said get out."

While David stomped away, Hannah gripped the scrub brush so hard her knuckles burned. The house, the kitchen, her promise—it all felt like more of a prison than the one Adeline had been in. She should go back to that scene with this suffocating feeling and bring Adeline's captivity to life.

But Adeline had been taken prisoner whereas Hannah wasn't physically trapped. This was her home, the place she was supposed to want to be. Her home was her life. She couldn't escape the drudgery of this life except by death or time. The former wasn't an option, so she was stuck with the latter.

The girls' laughter carried across the yard. Her sweet sisters. She shouldn't think of serving them as drudgery. She couldn't let a little humiliation make her hope for death. Her discontent probably had more to do with her story than her surroundings. She should focus on writing the perfect ending, not on wishing her life with her family to end.

"Are you all right?" her father asked from the porch, his forehead shiny with sweat.

She hadn't noticed him approaching. "I'm fine."

"I heard you yell at David."

"Sorry," she said without meaning it. David deserved to be yelled at and more. She returned her eyes to the floor as she scrubbed.

He unbuttoned his cuffs and rolled up his sleeves. "This is all my fault."

The scratching sound from her brush bristles echoed in the kitchen. "Father, it was my mistake. I went out in the storm. But I'm fine. I wish everyone would forget about it."

"I should have seen this coming. You're a grown woman. It's hard for a father to recognize that sometimes." A pained smile curved his lips. "Do you love Henry?"

How could she answer her father when she didn't know what these feelings were? He'd awakened something in her heart, attracted her even. But love? Wasn't falling in love supposed to be enjoyable? It was in every story she'd ever read.

Whatever was between her and Henry was too complicated to be enjoyable. Yet, just as he'd said at the springs, it was too important to ignore. She shrugged, hoping nonchalance would deter any more questions, at least until she had the answers herself. "I'm trying to take care of this household and finish my…" She stopped before she could say *story*. The completed story was supposed to be a surprise for her father. "I have too much work to do to worry about Henry. He's busy too."

Christopher took off his wide-brimmed hat. "He spoke with me last night after he brought you home. Asked permission to court you."

"Did he?" The words slipped from her mouth on a breath. She should have seen that coming. The way he'd looked at her the day he kissed her at the springs, his sitting by her at church, his risking his life to save her from the flooding cave. Their relationship hadn't felt like what she expected a real romance to feel like, but now he'd come to her father. He was making it real. Too real. For her and for her family. "Is that what has David so upset?"

Christopher shook his head. "Henry and I spoke alone. David doesn't know."

Henry was more serious than she'd thought. If he'd spoken to her father, he must think he had a future with her. Hadn't she told him she was committed to raising her sisters and taking care of her family? Why would he pursue her?

The feelings that overwhelmed her at the springs stirred again in her heart. No matter what feelings clouded her mind, she couldn't forget her promise. Nor could she deny her heart. She mindlessly scrubbed the same spot. "What was your answer… to Henry?"

"He has my blessing, Hannah, but it's up to you."

CHAPTER SEVENTEEN

Henry hung another freshly printed page onto the drying line at the back of his shop and examined the print. With precisely placed letters in perfect rows he'd replicated the last page of *The Gospel According to Luke*. Only one month into the elders' assignment and he'd printed over a quarter of the New Testament.

He'd worked six long days a week and would have to maintain the pace for three more months to complete the task in time. It would be a task easily accomplished if he could keep his mind focused. When he'd accepted the challenge of producing an error free copy of the New Testament, printed and bound by Good Springs's eighth anniversary celebration, he hadn't imagined he would want to court someone.

Hannah Vestal wasn't just someone.

She was creative and beautiful and captured his mind, finding her way into his every thought. He hadn't seen her all week, and it was bothering him. If his intellect were overcome by any more emotion, he might find himself desperately in love. He had to see her. It was illogical.

She would be working in her father's house, tending to the needs of six other people. He could see her at church on Sundays, but they couldn't speak to each other during the service and wouldn't have a moment alone afterward. How could he come to understand her if he didn't talk with her?

She'd said she spent her free hours on Sunday afternoons writing. He couldn't take that away from her. If he were going to see her, he would have to leave the press during the week and go to her. That would put his work behind schedule. If he didn't finish the elders' assignment on time, the printing press would not become a village-supported trade. He would have to hunt and fish and grow vegetables until he could produce and trade enough books to earn a living.

With a library to fill, he'd thought that life unacceptable. His father agreed.

Perhaps a short break in the afternoons wouldn't set him too far behind on his assignment. Not every afternoon, only now and then. Starting with now.

After a quick wipe of his hands, he untied his leather apron. As he reached to hang it on a peg on the wall, a dull thud hit the dusty floor in the doorway across the shop. He rounded the worktable and found a rock with a scrap of paper fastened to it with twine. The note read: *Leave hannah alone or you will regret it.*

He leaned out the open doorway. His father was standing at the top of the chapel's stone steps, talking to Reverend Colburn who was holding a broom. Both men laughed at something one of them said. Children's voices drifted from a porch down the road. Mr. Owens was driving his buckboard south toward his farm. No one else was around.

Henry read the note a second time. The message was meant to serve as a threat, but a perpetrator who threw rocks and ran didn't evoke fear, only annoyance.

The note writer wanted to keep him from Hannah and had assumed he would be easily bullied. That person hadn't been there when he'd saved Hannah from the floodwaters. The note writer underestimated the determination that simmered beneath this printer's scarred surface.

Henry's aching fist tightened around the slip of paper. He marched across the road to the chapel and caught his father's eye. "May I speak with you, Father?"

Matthew met him at the bottom of the stone steps. "What is it, son?"

"Did you see anyone run past the shop?"

"When?"

"A moment ago."

"No, but I wasn't looking." Matthew shielded his eyes from the sunlight and glanced up the stairs at Reverend Colburn who was sweeping the chapel's doorway. "William, did you see anyone run past the print shop a moment ago?"

The reverend shook his head and resumed his sweeping.

Matthew pointed at the note in Henry's hand. "Is something wrong?"

Henry checked the road. Though no one else was within earshot, he led his father across the road and into the print shop. He passed the note to his father. "This is the second time someone has anonymously warned me to keep away from Hannah."

Matthew widened his pale eyes at the note. "Seems childish. And sloppily written."

"Then we are agreed."

"Who do you think wrote it?"

"A child. Well, someone who is not anymore but is acting like one."

"Who?"

Henry remembered what Hannah said about her brother David not wanting them together. "A person who doesn't think I should court Hannah."

One corner of Matthew's lips curved into a grin, puffing his wooly side whiskers. "That list might be longer than you think."

"What do you mean?"

Matthew handed him back the note. "Well, you've had a few bad passes at courting. Might have left some hard feelings in your wake. Maybe someone doesn't want to see you break another heart."

Henry tossed the note onto the worktable. "It almost sounds like you're in agreement with them."

"Not fully." Matthew picked lint from his sleeves. "Men often take longer to commit than the fairer sex, but with a sweet girl like Hannah, you must be careful you aren't leading her down a road you don't want to travel."

At this point he was farther down that road than Hannah seemed to be. While he was focused on her, she was focused on the story she was writing. He paced to the window and looked toward the back of the schoolhouse where they'd danced that night. "That isn't the problem."

Matthew came beside him. "Then what is?"

When he didn't answer, his father patted his back. "I suggest you slow your pursuit until you are certain of your heart. Don't offer her something unless you are fully committed. It's too small of a village and Hannah is too sweet a girl." He stepped to the door to leave. "You are under the pressure of the elders' challenge and shouldn't stop your work to chase butterflies."

Henry watched Matthew walk away. His father was right. His time was already committed. Even though he'd spent many days imagining how love and marriage and a family might improve his life, he would only hurt Hannah if he pursued her when he didn't have time to offer more.

He rubbed the stiff scars of his left hand. Maybe someday they could court, but for now it wasn't reasonable for either of them. The only affection he should pursue was his first love—printing.

CHAPTER EIGHTEEN

Hannah reached between the cold prison bars for the figure in the dark. Before she saw his face, she could feel Aric's strong spirit. A string of opalescent pearls dangled at her wrist beneath her puffed velvet sleeves—a gift from the prince. She was Adeline.

The tall, attractive figure stepped into the light, thinning the shadows on his unshaven face. Between the bars he clasped her hand and kissed her forehead. "I've found you at last." He held up the jailor's keys. "Your freedom, my love."

The jangle of iron keys echoed through her stone cell. He unlocked the prison door, and it swung wide with a rusty creak. She wrapped her arms around his neck. "You never gave up on me!"

"I never will."

"What came of the battle?"

"The slave traders have been defeated." He knelt to unlock the chains cuffed around her ankles. "Their victims are free."

"And the kingdoms?"

"Reunited. Father abdicated, and I am king." A proud grin warmed his expression. "The kingdom is mine, but I would not be pleased to rule without you by my side. Marry me, Adeline, for you were born to be my queen."

Her breath caught on the magnitude of his words, but before she could answer, he kissed her. As he pulled away, her eyelids fluttered open. Instead of Aric, it was Henry who stood before her. Her sleeves were now a flower-print cotton fabric. Henry was her prince, her rescuer, her true love all along.

She traced a finger along his stubble-covered jaw, but instead of feeling whiskers, she felt something soft but lifeless.

Hannah opened her eyes and stilled her fingers, which were stroking her pillowcase.

She rolled onto her back in the bed she shared with Doris and sighed. That was the perfect ending to her story—not the part of the prince turning into Henry—before that. Aric should rescue Adeline, declare his love, and together they will rule the kingdom, happily ever after.

She checked the miniature clock on her desk beside the bed. Half past one. She'd only slept two hours. The feel of the story was as fresh in her mind as the kiss her dream prince had placed upon her lips. She had to write.

Moving in careful increments, she slid her feet to the floor. Doris let out a little hum in her sleep. Hannah glanced at her sister in the dark as she quietly opened her desk drawer. Once she'd gathered her paper and pencil, she tiptoed to the kitchen and lit the lamp on the table.

By dawn, her eyelids felt as heavy as Adeline's chains had been, but just like her heroine, she was free. The story was complete and the ending perfect. She read over the final pages once more to check for errors then tucked it back into her desk drawer as her sister stirred.

The routine of her morning—cooking for her family, washing dishes, assigning chores to her sisters—blurred in a haze of fondness for her completed story, pride in her accomplishment, and overwhelming affection for Henry Roberts.

She'd spent as much time sorting through her feelings for him as she had spent writing her story. Now the story was complete, and her feelings were clear. She loved Henry, and he had influenced her writing more than he knew. Desperation to show him the story added urgency to her every task.

She should take the pages to Olivia to be edited before she showed Henry. Not only had Olivia kindly critiqued her story thus far, but also she would edit it. Hannah had assured Henry the final copy would be edited. But if Olivia was busy, it might be several days before Henry would have the privilege of reading it. And several days before she had the privilege of accepting his praise after he'd read it.

Maybe she could edit it herself.

She grabbed a dust rag from the shelf above the washtub to appear to be working and hurried to her desk in the corner of her and Doris's bedroom. The girls had gone to clean the coop, and only her father was still in the house, repairing his fishing net in the mudroom. She scanned the final pages and didn't see a single mistake. She could always show Olivia the story later. Maybe she'd even surprise her with a printed and bound copy.

The fear of having others read her work dissolved in the certainty that the story was strong—better than strong. It was everything a love story should be. Soon, she would have Henry's approval, which would validate her efforts. Then he would turn her story into a beautiful book.

She imagined giving her father the book on his fiftieth birthday. She would roast a chicken for dinner and bake apples for dessert. Then, after her siblings had given him their presents, she would kneel before him, tell him how much his guidance had encouraged her writing, and present him with the book. No, no. She would give it to him on his birthday morning before anyone else was up, so he would have the day to relish her gift before the others presented theirs. He would be so proud of her. Though thrilled with the notion of seeing Henry, this book business was for her father.

She gathered all one hundred ninety-six pages, tied them with twine, and tucked them into her satchel. Forgetting about the dust rag, she carried the satchel to a basket of candles on the storage shelves in the kitchen. She made sure her father could see what she was doing and slid a few candles in the satchel. "I need to go into the village for a while. I have to trade these for paper."

Christopher glanced at her then returned his gaze to his net mending. "Trade with Henry?"

"Of course." She was trading the candles as part of their arrangement for the book's printing, but she couldn't let her father know it. "Henry has the paper and cutting board."

Her father gave her a knowing grin. Was it because of Henry or had he caught her dishonesty? The trade for paper wasn't necessary. She closed her satchel and tied its flap securely. "You were the one who told me to write. You said you wanted to see me use my God-given talents."

"And I meant it." He shifted out of the doorway as she descended the mudroom steps. "Be back by lunch."

"I will."

She hoisted the satchel's strap over her head to let the bag hang across her body as she scurried through the yard. The morning grass wet her hem, but she didn't care. The warm sun flickered off the dew across the pasture. She looked to the side of the property where her mother was buried. The stone marker stood beyond the incline. Though it wasn't visible from the path to the road, she whispered in its direction. "I finally finished it, Mama. It's perfect."

The vacant road into the village welcomed her with its soft morning haze. A jackrabbit sat at the road's edge across from the Cotters' house, chewing its breakfast. Birds chattered in the grass and underbrush and the gray leaf trees above. The stately trees reached their limbs across the road to lace their leaves with one another high above the lane.

Hannah almost hummed as she walked the road into the village, but that seemed more like something Doris would do. Her completed story gave her a taste of freedom. Perhaps that was why carefree girls like Doris hummed and twirled; only their ribbons weighed them down.

The print shop door stood open, and a rhythmic tapping came from inside. Hannah smoothed her hair and straightened her posture as she walked to the doorway. Scant light hazed the north-facing window near Henry's letterpress. The candles she'd traded to him last month burned brightly in the center of the shop. It took a moment for her eyes to adjust to the low light after being outside.

Henry's back faced the door as he leaned over the letterpress, tapping a little tool against a row of type. He turned a degree when she stepped inside. His brow was furrowed with annoyance but relaxed the instant he saw her.

"Hannah," he said closing the distance between them. "What a delightful surprise."

"I brought you something."

He tossed his little tool to the worktable beside them. It landed at the base of a candelabrum that held a triplet of burning tapers. He rubbed the back of his neck, looking hopeful and boyish. "Something for me?"

She opened her satchel and first drew out the candles she'd brought, setting them on the worktable two at a time, wanting to build suspense. "These are the beginning of my payment."

The hope drained from his expression as he glanced from her to the candles and back again. "Payment?"

"Yes, you remember our agreement." She lowered her volume. "More candles in exchange for printing my story."

"Oh." He moved a hand to the worktable. She expected him to touch the candles, but instead he straightened a stack of his finely printed pages. Once the pages were perfectly aligned, he picked up his tool and thumped it against the palm of his good hand.

Hoping she'd misread his disappointment, she continued her coy presentation. "I brought the first part of my payment because… even though it is two months early…" she almost squealed with excitement as she drew out the completed manuscript, "my story is ready to be printed."

She waited for him to gasp from surprise at her efficiency or wrap her in his arms and profess his pride in her and his love for her. He only stared at the manuscript and kept thumping the tool against his palm.

She took a half step forward and slid the twine-bound pages onto the worktable next to the candelabrum. "I thought you would be... rather... aren't you pleased?"

His Adam's apple raised and lowered as he swallowed. "Yes, of course, I'm pleased for you. You set out to finish your story and achieved just that."

Perhaps she was being oversensitive about his reaction because she'd only slept two hours last night. Maybe she'd expected too much from him. He'd given no indication he was the sort of man who celebrated such accomplishments. Still, didn't human decency dictate he should at least congratulate her?

She'd probably surprised him too much. Some men needed a few moments to process news. She cast her gaze about the room to give him time to conjure a response worthy of the interest he'd claimed to possess for her. Her eyes moved from the letterpress to the cabinet of thin drawers to the window with the view of the stone library next door.

He said nothing.

She picked up her bound manuscript and flashed him a smile. "The ending came to me in a dream. I've never written anything so quickly in my life."

He glanced back at the letterpress. "Hannah, I'm pleased with your efficiency, however, this is quite unexpected. I didn't think we would have to do this for a couple of months."

What did he mean *have to do this*? He'd been apprehensive about her writing ability at first, but since the dance he'd seemed smitten with her. Didn't admiring a person extend to their creations? This story was, after all, as much a part of her as her eyes and voice. She proffered the manuscript. "Don't you want to read it?"

He pressed his lips together. "I won't have time to read the whole story until my project for the elders is complete. But I believe a final page can reveal the merit of a work." He laid the manuscript on the worktable and untied the twine. "And since you're especially proud of the story's ending, you should have no problem with me reading only that much for now."

Her heart skipped from both delight and devastation that he would read her words. She took a deep breath as he flipped the manuscript over and selected the last page. He leaned against the worktable and held the page close to the candlelight as he read. She walked to the window unable to watch him read her work.

The taut silence in the room broke when he shifted his weight away from the worktable. He returned the page to its place in her manuscript. "Is this your best work?"

She walked toward him, ignoring the sickly feeling produced by her fluttering heart. "I believe it is, yes."

He thumped his little tool against his palm once more and went back to work at his letterpress. He tapped the letter row with the tool. "The ending is trite. It's ample sign the story is not ready for binding, much less printing. I suggest you work on it more."

Hannah stared at his back, his words pricking her ears like bee stings. How could he throw out criticism so flippantly then go back to his work as if he'd commented on humidity or stale bread? Her story was not so trivial as hot weather or old food. This story was her lifeblood and writing it had carried her through years of pain and loneliness. Her fists clenched so tightly her fingernails dug into her palms. "How dare you!"

He barely took his focus off his type long enough to flick a glance at her. "Don't take it personally, sweetheart."

Sweetheart? She wasn't his sweetheart and never would be if this was how he treated someone he cared for. She picked up the final page of her manuscript and shook it at him. "You only read one page. You don't know the whole story."

"I read enough to know you chose an overused trope. It's a fairy tale romance."

"It is not!"

He straightened his spine, blowing out an impatient breath. "You have a prince rescuing his love interest, declaring his love for her, and suggesting they will rule the kingdom happily ever after."

"So?"

"So, he is returning from a battle where he fought the slave trade. That would leave the kingdoms filled with wounded and scarred individuals. He is reuniting two kingdoms. That would come with political problems. His father is abdicating the throne. That would cause family turmoil and palace chaos. You have ignored the logical consequences of your plot's complications and instead tied up the story with a romantic happy ending. You might as well sprinkle in a few magic beans because it's a fairy tale."

"It is a love story."

"Sentiment isn't believable. A reader's trust is built by the author's logic. The ending is illogical, and therefore I must assume the rest of the story is too."

"How could you be so heartless? You're convinced everything you do is worthwhile, but you criticized my whole work harshly after only reading one page."

"One crucial page."

"Are you even capable of loving anyone but yourself?"

He froze with his lips parted and pierced her with his sapphire gaze.

She didn't care that she'd offended him after the way he'd judged her story. She grabbed her manuscript and stuffed it into her satchel without bothering to tie it first. "I knew you would be a stern critic, but I also thought you would be happy for me. I thought you might show some respect for my hard work even if it wasn't to your taste. I thought you would—" Keeping her eyes on him, she reached back to grab the candles she'd brought to trade. Her hand bumped the candelabrum, knocking its three burning tapers onto a stack of his printed pages, setting them ablaze. She gasped.

Henry jumped toward the worktable and beat the fire with his leather apron. "What have you done?" His voice bellowed like the roar of a crazed animal as he swatted the flames. "You ruined a month's worth of work!"

Her voice seized up. She couldn't have replied if she'd wanted to. Smoke stung her crying eyes. She hugged her satchel to her chest and ran out of the print shop, weeping.

CHAPTER NINETEEN

Henry slammed his fist into the heap of charred pages on his worktable. Ash flew into the smoky air. "More than half of my pages are ruined! What am I supposed to do now, Father? What?"

Matthew calmly brushed a hand broom over the worktable, whisking ash and remnants of Henry's work into a dustpan. "Now, son, this is nothing you can't handle—a mere setback. Roberts men have fought fires and infestations and dripping roofs in our print shops for generations. No flame nor storm nor pest can stop our presses."

Losing the pages fueled only half of Henry's anger; his quarrel with Hannah fueled the rest. He ground his teeth until they ached. "I never should have gotten involved with her."

"The fire was an accident." Matthew's eyebrows arched high, sending a wave of deep wrinkles through his forehead. "Let's not blame the girl."

"I don't. I blame myself." He glared down at the mess. "Almost a month's work wasted."

"On the printing project or on Hannah?" Matthew held the dustpan outside the open door and knocked the ashes into the wind. As he returned to the worktable, he caught Henry's eye as if expecting an answer.

When Henry said nothing, his father whistled one long flat note. "I see. If you have committed to pursuing Miss Vestal, go to her and beg forgiveness. No woman in love can resist a sincere apology from her suitor."

If only it were that simple. He hadn't wronged her by doing something he ought not do but by being true to his principles. What would he say in his apology? That from now on he would ignore his professional standards, forgo logic, and swallow his truthful opinions? What would be left of him then? A shell of a man. A printer who produced volume after volume of rot. A spineless romantic with an overflowing library from which no one with a modicum of intelligence would want to read.

Once again, a woman had asked too much of him. He shook his throbbing head. "She wants something I cannot give." He motioned to the blackened pages. "You needn't worry yourself with this, Father."

"You're right. This is your print shop now." Matthew laid the hand broom and dustpan on the table and held up both palms in surrender. "Forgive me for trying to clean your mess."

Henry turned his back on the burnt pages and looked out the window. The empty stone library next door stared back, mocking him. He didn't think it would be this difficult. "I should tell the elders tonight."

"No meeting tonight, son. Tomorrow is Christmas Eve and the men want to spend time with their families."

"Doesn't feel like Christmas."

Matthew scratched his white side whiskers. "Never does to me, not since moving to the southern hemisphere. Warm Christmases and snowy Junes. Seems unnatural after so many years of my life spent on the other side of the earth."

Henry blew out a breath. "Those born in the Land will never know the difference."

"Those born in the Land will never know a great many things," Matthew motioned toward the building next door, "especially if the shelves of our library remain empty."

As if anger and frustration were not enough, his father was ladling guilt into the cesspool of self-loathing already churning within Henry. Why did people think they could appeal to a man's logic by trying to force more emotions upon him? Perhaps it worked on lesser intelligent men. He'd had his fill of conversation for the day.

He returned to the worktable, scooped up the last of the ruined pages, and carried them to the stone fireplace in the back corner of the cabin where the previous tenants once cooked their meals. With the strike of a match, all physical evidence of Hannah's accident was gone. If only the fracture in their relationship could be fixed as easily.

It couldn't.

He stood from the hearth and straightened his spine. "Thank you for stopping in, Father, but I'm quite determined to get back to work."

"That's the boy." Matthew smiled, flashing his porcelain false teeth. "I'll be at my paper-making station in the barn at home if you need anything. If we don't see you by supper, I shall send Ellenore with a plate."

Henry didn't want to see anyone for the rest of the day, even his favorite sister. He dusted his hands together. "I'd rather be alone."

"Very well, son," Matthew turned to leave, taking his good intentions with him.

Henry leaned against the worktable for a moment. Then he checked out the door to make sure he was alone. His father had already passed the library and was almost to the schoolhouse on the road home. No one else was in sight. Smoke billowed from the chimney of the Owenses' smokehouse, and the scent of venison filled the air.

He'd had enough of smoke for the day too.

Stepping back into his shop, he lifted the little glass lantern Dr. Ashton had given him. He sniffed the strange fuel. He'd been so determined not to use the light source since highly flammable oil fueled it, but candles had done enough damage, not only by their fire ruining his pages, but also by his need to trade with Hannah to obtain them.

He lit the lantern's wick and turned the dial as Dr. Ashton had demonstrated. A white-hot flame with a blue center grew and cast its light across the shop.

He set the lantern on his letter cabinet near the press and opened the drawer where he kept the plans for each page. Beneath the plans was the sketch of Mrs. Susanna Vestal. He'd brought it to the shop intending to show Hannah next time she came to trade candles. Before he'd been able to show her the only existing image of her late mother, she'd shown him the last page of her completed manuscript.

Ghastly story it was too, or must be to have such an ending. Every word he'd said to her about it had been true. If their positions were reversed, he would have wanted to hear the truth. So why had she become so offended?

There was the crux of his loneliness; he did not understand the fairer sex nor ever would. His sisters were easy enough to please. They simply wanted courteous men and generous compliments. His mother was the same but also required the occasional display of gratitude. Above all, the women in his family seemed to value honesty, especially Ellenore, which was why they preferred each other. She wanted his honest opinions, and he respected her for it.

But not the girls he tried to court.

They wanted flattery, constant approbation, and a man who lived to engage in petty placation.

Well, he wasn't the right man for them—any of them, especially Hannah Vestal. He looked into the eyes on the sketch. They were Hannah's eyes. He couldn't bear to look at it another moment. He slid the sketch back into the cabinet then stood by the window, staring northward. The scarred tendons beneath the lumpy skin of his left hand stung, so he curled and stretched his fist as he stared out the window. It didn't relieve the pain.

He'd known this would happen with Hannah. He'd tried to warn her. Neither of them had listened. He'd thought loving a woman might improve his life, but it had not.

Though a hollow pit in his chest ached and always would, Hannah Vestal was better off without him.

CHAPTER TWENTY

Hannah stared at the gutter of her open Bible for the length of the Sunday service. Beside her, Minnie and Ida fidgeted on the pew, but she didn't care to correct them. Occasionally, her father's hand would still whichever twin became too wiggly.

Reverend Colburn's authoritative voice filled the chapel like the hum of floodwaters. It reminded Hannah of the evening she'd been trapped behind the waterfall. Henry had saved her then; he had calmed her and led her to safety. He'd been different that night. She liked that side of him, but there was no bringing it back. After rejecting her story and humiliating her, she'd spent the better part of a week seething at the thought of Henry Roberts.

When the sermon ended, she couldn't have repeated a word of it, for Henry was sitting three rows behind her. She didn't need to look back to know he was there. She could sense him like one feels a storm coming before a single cloud has formed. And like a storm, Henry had blown into her life with his wit and confidence and left her reeling from the same.

She may have accidentally started the small fire that burned a few papers in his shop, but he was the betrayer. She'd believed him when he'd said whatever was between them was too important to ignore. She'd trusted him with her heart—not that they had confessed their love for one another, but she opened her soul to him by sharing her writing.

His reaction to her writing was the most severe point of his betrayal. She'd trusted him with her story, and he'd flippantly scanned one page before declaring the whole work rubbish. Maybe he deserved to have some of his papers burned.

No, even though he'd hurt her she didn't want his work to be ruined.

When the reverend dismissed the congregation, Hannah's father stood. Both of the twins shot to their feet with the sudden realization they were free to move. They squeezed past Hannah and Wade to get out of the pew. Hannah didn't stop them.

She glanced at Wade as he shuffled between the pews to the aisle with her. "I'm surprised you didn't sit with Ben and Judah today."

Wade shrugged, not listening. His gaze was fixed on someone a few rows back.

She followed his line of sight to the one man who was standing still in the moving crowd at the back of the chapel. Henry looked away as soon as their eyes met. If only she'd been the one to look away first.

Wade scowled at Henry.

Hannah nudged him. "Would you stop that, please?"

"I want him to leave you alone."

"You needn't worry about that."

Wade faced her and seemed less like the boy she'd helped raise and more like a man. His fists were balled so tightly his knuckles were white. "I'll always worry about you if someone wants to court you."

She adjusted the ribbons on her church bonnet. "Well, he doesn't want to, and no one else in the settlement has ever been interested in me, so your worrying is needless."

Wade's hands relaxed. "Good."

As Christopher walked ahead of them toward the chapel door, Hannah waved to Doris and the twins. "Come along, girls." She tried to appear occupied with her sisters as they neared the back of the chapel where Henry stood talking to Gabe and Olivia, but for once none of the girls needed her attention. She hugged her Bible to her chest and pressed her fingers into the book's spine.

Her father greeted Henry and patted his shoulder as he passed. If she looked for long, they might make eye contact again. If they did, he might see the sadness looming behind any angry expression she'd be tempted to make. She looked at Olivia and Gabe, who had little Daniel hanging on to both of their hands.

Olivia held up a finger to Henry to pause their conversation. She reached for Hannah's arm, stopping her slow procession to the door. "Do you have anything… new to show me?" She followed her question about Hannah's writing with a secretive smile.

Hannah shook her head. "I won't have anything to show you for a while. Maybe never again." Her eyes moved without her permission to Henry's face. A flash of sorrow darkened his expression. He'd been so arrogant and then angry last time she saw him, she hadn't considered that he might regret his behavior. The hint of guilt seemed to vanish as quickly as it had come. He checked his pocket watch.

Olivia glanced between Hannah and Henry. Her porcelain forehead crinkled beneath wisps of straight black hair. "I'm sorry to hear that."

Minnie pulled on Hannah's sleeve. "I'm hungry."

Hannah smoothed her little sister's hair then forced a smile for Olivia. "It's for the best. My time is committed to my family. I wasted too much of it on... that diversion."

Her father and Wade were standing at the door waiting, so she walked on. She glanced back as she left the church with her family. Olivia and Gabe were exchanging a concerned look. Henry was already speaking with someone else. After all she'd been through, he wasn't affected at all. She'd meant nothing to him.

A cloak of numbness shrouded Hannah as she walked home with her family. It didn't matter that the warm sun had ignited summertime in the Land with lush foliage, swooping songbirds, and fragrant wildflowers blossoming in every meadow. It didn't matter that she had her family's love and approval. She had lost someone close to her. Again.

She slowed her pace as she approached the house. David and Wade flung the back door open, eager to get out of their cravats and waistcoats. The twins raced inside, knocking into each other as they climbed the mudroom steps. Doris twirled once then stood on tiptoe to kiss Christopher's cheek before walking inside.

Christopher stayed on the stoop, holding the door open for Hannah. "Are you all right?"

"I'm fine," she mumbled.

"You've been dragging your feet for days. What's wrong?"

She turned her face into the wind that blew across the meadow where her mother was buried. The tall grass bent in pulsing waves. In summers past, she imagined it was her mother's way of waving to her. Not anymore. Her imagination was no longer her friend.

Neither was Henry Roberts.

Christopher tried again. "Does this have anything to do with your candle trade at the print shop the other day?"

She snapped her attention away from the meadow. "I don't want to talk about it."

"I wish you had a mother for these times."

"I don't want *a* mother," she said as she stopped near the stoop. "I miss *my* mother."

"I know, sweet Hannah, I know. I only meant you would benefit from the advice of a woman." He lowered his chin. "Maybe you should visit Olivia one day this week to have someone to talk to. A feminine perspective. She has the gift of encouragement. She encouraged me after your mother's passing, and it affected me deeply."

She shook her head. She didn't want anyone's encouragement or any more talk of gifts. She'd taken their advice to use her *gift* of writing, and with one sharp critique, Henry had drained all the enjoyment out of her only solace—her writing.

She'd also followed Olivia's advice to take her story to Henry to be printed. Olivia had assured her Henry would be fair—maybe not pleasant but fair, she'd said. Olivia wasn't to blame for Henry's behavior; in Olivia's experience Henry might have been a fair judge of writing. Maybe he was right. Maybe it was a terrible story.

With one breath from someone else's lungs, her only happiness was gone.

If she didn't have her writing and she didn't have her mother, what was left? Cleaning and mending and making candles and soap? Feeding six people who only saw her back as she stood at the stove for hours each day?

The mindless work of the home was all she had. It was the least she could do for her father since she wouldn't be granting his request and letting him read her story. She had tried to use her writing to bless others, and all she'd done was failed. She'd failed her father and Olivia and her characters... and Henry. Her throat tightened, but she would not cry. Not now. She didn't look at Christopher as she passed him and stepped into the noisy kitchen.

CHAPTER TWENTY-ONE

Henry sat between his father and Gabe for the last elders' meeting of the year. He squelched a yawn as Reverend Colburn gave each elder the floor to address his family's business. The elders' firstborn sons sat quietly, observing the ways they were expected to continue one day. After working late into the night at the letterpress for several days, Henry's mind refused to focus during the tedious meeting.

He would obey the settlement's rules and fulfill his duty as an elder in Good Springs one day, but it didn't make sense considering his fate. The purpose of a family's elder was to represent his family's business. Henry was doomed to live alone.

Therefore, committing to become an elder was illogical. Thanks to the fire last week, his goal with the New Testament printing was improbable. And his delusion he could love Hannah well and maybe have a family of his own someday was impractical.

Illogical. Improbable. Impractical.

This is what he'd become. A failure. The word was hard to swallow, and it might well be true about him. As

Mr. Foster returned to his seat and Reverend Colburn called on Matthew to give an update of the Roberts family's business, Henry straightened his posture. A failure he might be, but he need not let on in public.

Matthew strode to the front of the room and drew a folded piece of gray leaf paper from his breast pocket. "I've traded paper to the McIntoshes for the building of twenty-four drying racks, which has doubled my paper production abilities. I'll have ample paper supply for the new school year, and should anyone wish to trade for paper, my family is in need of thread, yarn, and cloth." He glanced up from his paper and chuckled. "My daughters aren't keen on weaving or spinning."

Henry didn't laugh. His sisters had plenty of work to do already. The more workers who specialized in one product like his father had and quickly produced goods, the more the settlement would be free to flourish.

Matthew finished detailing their family's settlement business and nodded once at Reverend Colburn. Before Matthew could take his seat, the reverend raised his hand. "What about the printing press? Give us an update on Henry's progress with the New Testament."

Matthew looked at Henry and scratched his side whiskers. "My son is putting his full effort into the project, working dawn to midnight most days. There was a setback recently, a small fire. But I'm quite sure Henry will meet the challenge."

The elders glanced at each other at the mention of a fire. Christopher Vestal's brow furrowed with concern. He asked Matthew, "Was anyone hurt?"

For once Henry was glad he wasn't being addressed about his own business. If he were, he'd have to answer honestly. Yes, someone was hurt in the incident—not by the blaze but by his attitude.

"No, no," Matthew answered quickly. "Only a few pages lost. No matter. Henry has already reprinted many of them."

As Matthew returned to his seat, Christopher looked at Henry. Unable to discern the meaning behind Christopher's stoic expression, Henry pressed his lips together and turned his gaze to the reverend. Still, he could feel Christopher looking at him.

Did the father of the woman he loved know he'd hurt her feelings? Did Christopher know Hannah had started the fire? Did he know their relationship was ruined?

It didn't matter anymore.

Henry's every hope of improving his life went up in the smoke from Hannah's fire. He wasn't able to love a woman well. He'd hurt Hannah and didn't deserve her. It was time he accepted the life of a failure. He would pass the eldership to Simon, sleep on a cot at the back of the print shop, and die alone.

CHAPTER TWENTY-TWO

By late January, the long summer days of the southern hemisphere were shortening, which suited Hannah just fine. The sooner the day was over, the sooner she could crawl back into bed and escape her misery by sleeping. Gone were her afternoons of dreaming up stories and secretly scribbling notes, her evenings of joy while the anticipation to write built, and her quiet late night writing sessions. Now, without the tourniquet of writing, each day bled into the next like a fatal wound.

Hannah filled a clean bucket at the well then scanned the horizon as she carried the water into the house. The sun sank behind the trees to the west, leaving the sky full of golden clouds stacked to the heavens. The air flowing into the mudroom cooled the kitchen as it blew the heat of cooking out the open front door.

Another dinner eaten, another day gone.

Her family had settled into their evening routine with her father sitting in the parlor reading his Bible, Doris poking at her needlework by the lantern, and the twins playing on the rug with their ever-growing seashell collection. David whittled on the front porch while Wade wrestled with the puppies.

Hannah set the water bucket by the kitchen sink then studied her family. Though they all looked content, the veil of her sadness kept her from joining them.

There was nothing particularly unpleasant about her life. Her family had more than they needed, and she had a good life caring for them. It was in the still moments where she found her mind racing in desperation to change her circumstances while her heart ached too much to do anything about it.

She missed her stories, missed discussing her writing with Olivia, missed Henry. Her only companion now was her desperation for escape.

Perhaps God would relieve her suffering and allow her to be inflicted with the same ailment that took her mother's life, so she could die in her thirties as well. Only a decade to go and she could join her mother in Glory. The morbid thought almost brought happiness—the first twinge of joy she'd felt since Henry had dashed her love of writing and her hope for love.

She untied her apron and stepped out the back door to loosen the crumbs from it. With the first shake of the apron, a folded-up slip of paper flung into the air and landed in the grass near the stoop. She knew better than to open it, but her fingers unfolded it anyway.

Pencil markings covered the page with notes for a love letter she'd planned to have Prince Aric send Adeline in her story. She'd left the vowels out of each word to disguise the meaning in case one of her siblings had found the note and assumed she had written it to a man or a man had written it to her.

That would never happen now.

Ripping the paper again and again, she yearned to feel the way she'd felt when Henry was intrigued with her. He'd never said he loved her, but he'd looked at her like she was captivating. Whatever had been between them was undeniable.

It was care and desire and interest and attraction. And she'd barely had a chance to enjoy it before it was over.

Maybe it wasn't real. Maybe she'd imagined it too. Maybe she'd been so engrossed in her story she had projected the feelings she created for her characters into real life.

A salty tear slid between her lips as she held the tiny squares of ripped paper in her hands.

No, her feelings for Henry were real.

She'd admired him very much—loved him even. She'd wanted to know everything about him and spend more time with him, even to the point of imagining shirking her promise to her mother. How could she not see it was love before it fell apart?

As she sat on the stoop holding the tiny bits of paper, Wade led the puppies from the front of the house to the barn. A moment later he closed the barn doors and walked back to the house. He eyed her as he passed by and stepped into the mudroom, but she turned her face away. His boots clunked as they hit the floor, then he plodded through the kitchen. At least he didn't say anything about her crying. Maybe he hadn't noticed in the low light of nightfall.

Male voices murmured lightly in the parlor at the other end of the kitchen. Then, footsteps descended the mudroom steps behind her. She didn't look back but closed her cupped hands over the ripped note.

Christopher stepped out to the stoop with his feet bare and closed the door behind him. He sat beside her. Without a word he held an open palm in front of her as a parent does when they expect a child to give them a broken toy.

Tears blurred her vision as she poured the bits of torn paper into her father's waiting hand.

He closed his fingers over the sad confetti and withdrew a clean handkerchief from his shirt pocket. He kept his caring voice low. "Was this a letter from Henry?"

"No." She wiped her eyes. "It was for my story."

He angled his chin. "Are you still writing?"

"No."

"Are you and Henry still friends?"

"No."

"Did one affect the other?"

When she said nothing, he turned his face toward the barn across the yard. "I had a feeling."

"At least you have feelings. Henry doesn't. I thought he did at first, but he only cares about his printing."

"He is under tremendous pressure from the elders right now. Reverend Colburn assigned him a task too big for any man." He nudged her softly. "I'll let you in on a secret. For the elders, it isn't so much completing the assignment that matters, but how Henry handles it."

"He told me about having to print a copy of the New Testament in four months. He seemed busy but confident. Perhaps those characteristics will aide him in his assignment even if they make him a lousy suitor."

"So he asked you then?"

"Asked me what?"

"To court."

"We never got that far." She wished her mother were here to talk to. Her father cared, but how much should she tell him? As a man he might not understand the intricacies of feminine emotion. If he knew Henry had broken her heart, he might become angry with Henry. Or her.

She glanced at his profile. Her father was a man, but he was also a caring man who had raised six children alone. He'd proven his compassion time and again. She blotted her nose and wadded his handkerchief in a tight ball. "I needed Henry's opinion about something… something that matters a great deal to me. And he was very harsh."

"Harsh?"

"He ripped out my heart, threw it to the floor, and crushed it with his muddy boot."

She waited for Christopher's shocked response. When he said nothing, she looked at him.

His eyes were wide and his lips curved in a half-grin. "Henry did all that, did he?"

"Metaphorically, of course."

"Of course." Christopher held the bits of paper in one hand and leaned the other palm behind him on the stoop. "When your mother and I were first courting, before that even, she would get so angry with me over small things. Sometimes, I knew I'd befuddled my words and caused the trouble. Sometimes, I didn't have an inkling of my wrong. But that didn't stop her from being upset with me."

Most of Hannah's memories of her mother were of an ill and soft-tempered woman. Before Susanna's illness, her parents had always spoken kindly to one another. "I can't imagine Mother being ungracious to you."

Christopher leaned forward. "And that's just it. When we were courting, I never thought of Susanna as being ungracious. I knew nothing of the ways of women, and so I assumed it was my fault. Granted, I was young and foolish enough it was possible I was wrong in each circumstance."

He looked up as the first glints of starlight broke through the night sky. "I was happy to take the blame because I loved her."

Hannah's heart sank. "Then Henry doesn't love me. If he did, he would have made amends by now."

Her father raised a finger. "He has a different temperament than I do and has endured things I never have, so I can't claim to understand him. I watched him work the ship's sails for months during our voyage here. No matter the conditions, he was the first man at the ropes and the last man standing in a storm. He helped build most of the houses in this settlement until the accident. And now he works long hours each day at an intricate job with a hand that pains him." He shook his head. "Henry Roberts is not a man to be judged quickly."

She huffed. "No matter how quickly he judges?"

Christopher peeled his gaze from the stars. "Did he judge you harshly, Hannah, or did he give you the honest opinion you asked for?"

"Well, yes, but…" She couldn't tell her father this was about her writing without explaining she'd taken her story to be printed for his birthday. It would only sadden her father to know she'd failed him. "I feel as though he betrayed me."

"Did he?"

"He led me to believe I had a chance at something."

"A chance and a promise are two different things. Did he give you a chance at whatever this was?"

"Yes."

"So, he didn't mislead you?"

"Well, no."

Christopher's voice came in a near whisper. "The reason your mother and I kept courting was that she forgave me after every time she'd been upset with me. We were young and immature and her complaints against me were petty. But still the grace of God ruled in her heart and was growing in her to where each time we fought she forgave me quicker. Soon, she realized I truly loved her and she no longer became upset with me easily. Our courtship was difficult, but it was worth it. By the time we were married, she'd learned not to let the little things matter too much and not to let the right things matter too little."

She traced a finger in the dirt beside her feet and imagined Henry asking her for forgiveness. What would she want him to apologize for? For giving her his opinion of her writing when she'd asked him to? For not liking her story? Those weren't personal affronts. "Perhaps I'm like my mother."

"More than you will ever know." Christopher smiled. "I believe Henry to be a wise man or I wouldn't have given him my permission to court you. Try to put aside your anger and think about what upset you. It usually isn't the incorrect judgments that offend us, but those that contain some truth. Was there any truth to his words?"

Henry told her the story's ending was trite and illogical and she hadn't given it enough thought. She'd stayed up all night writing it and had been so excited to see Henry she hadn't taken her pages to Olivia to be edited, as she normally did… as she'd promised she would… as she should have.

Perhaps Henry was right.

The manuscript was tucked inside her desk drawer where it had remained untouched since their argument. Maybe she should reread those last few pages. What if Henry was only pushing her to work harder, to make the story better? She had reacted badly, ran out like a child, and buried her talent in the drawer.

Buried in a drawer, not buried in a grave. Since she was still breathing, God wanted her here. Though night had fallen, the surrounding darkness seemed to lift. She wiped her final tears and faced her father. "Henry's opinion was harsh but honest. And yes, I asked for it, so I shouldn't have faulted him. I fear our relationship is beyond repair now."

Christopher poured the little bits of paper back into her hand. "If he loves you, nothing is beyond repair."

"And if he doesn't?"

Her father gave her shoulder a squeeze as he stood. "Then the experience will give you something to write about."

After her father went inside, she looked up at the stars and prayed if God wanted her to write, He would rescue her from this despair.

A warm breeze blew through the orchard and reminded her of a scene in her story. The boldness she'd felt while writing filled her mind and brought with it the desire to reread her story. She should see if there was any truth to Henry's assessment.

Popping up from the stoop, she hurried into the house, through the kitchen, and into her bedroom. She sat at her desk and opened its drawer. There her manuscript hid, wrinkled and abandoned. She smoothed out the creases on the cover page and began reading.

CHAPTER TWENTY-THREE

Henry pinched a copper sort between his thumb and forefinger while he wiped it clean. His scarred hand ached, begging him to be done with work for the day. One by one he set the cleaned sorts neatly in their place in the letter cabinet. His work would be over for the day when he said so, not when the pain took hold.

Gabe stepped into the doorway of the print shop, holding a covered glass jar filled with black soot. "From Olivia."

"Excellent." Henry lifted his chin at the worktable. "Set it there."

"She said this would be the last jar of soot she can collect for a while since school is starting next week."

Henry glanced outside at the late summer sunset. The long hours he'd spent in the print shop had made the months blur. "So soon."

"She's having the younger children start class two weeks before the others this year. Thinks it will help them settle into the routine."

Henry wasn't in the mood to talk, let alone talk about other people's children. He would never have a family, never have children. He wouldn't need to know about sending them to school, only what books to print and how many copies. He pointed at the jar of soot. "Give your bride my thanks."

Gabe nodded and set down the jar. He rounded the worktable and began reading the uncut pages drying on the line. "Already at Ephesians?" He flashed a smile over his thick shoulder. "You might finish this project in time after all."

"Might."

"What will you work on next?"

He had planned to print Hannah's story if she fixed its flaws and had it ready. But in the six weeks since the fire, she hadn't come around the print shop and had barely given him a glance when he saw her at church. She didn't want his services after their argument, didn't want him at all. He tried to shrug off the hurt, but nothing helped. "The elders will tell me what to print. If the village is contributing to my support, I'll work on whatever is needed."

"Olivia is eager for you to print more story books," Gabe said as he lifted the lantern from the worktable and held it near the wet pages for a closer look. The bright oil-burning flame washed the page. "Not reprints of the books from America though. She was hoping for new stories to teach from. Perhaps something by a new writer here in Good Springs."

Henry wasn't taking the bait and talking about Hannah's writing. He continued cleaning the sorts despite the stiffness in his hand.

Gabe returned the lantern to its place and leaned down, propping his elbows on the worktable. "My father and I were at the Vestals' yesterday. Have you ever seen the pottery wheel Mrs. Vestal brought from Virginia?"

Henry glanced up. "Only when we were unloading the ship."

"Wade wants to learn to make pottery, even found some good clay to use. But Susanna never showed anyone how to work the pottery wheel. We all gave it a try, kicking the fly wheel and squeezing the clay." Gabe chuckled. "Wade got more frustrated with us by the minute. He didn't say anything. Mr. Vestal tried to mold the clay and keep the wheel spinning just right. I tried. Father tried. Finally, Wade got fed up with us flinging balls of clay across the barn. His cheeks were as red as that apple," he said pointing to the fruit Henry kept in a bowl on the shelf.

Henry put the last cleaned sort in the letter cabinet and closed the drawer with the heel of his hand. "What did Wade do?"

"Nothing. He stormed off and kicked a clump of clay on his way out of the barn."

Henry wiped his fingertips with the cloth. "It could happen to any of us."

"What could?"

"Die without teaching someone else what we know, leaving no instruction of our life's work." The notion stirred him. "We should do something about it before anyone else passes away and takes their profession with them."

"What can we do?"

"I must think about it. Our purpose in coming to unsettled land was to form a more civilized society, but if knowledge is lost, quality of life will regress for future generations."

Gabe nodded solemnly. "Or we will leave each other as frustrated as Wade was yesterday. I've always felt sorry for the Vestals since Susanna died."

"As have I."

"Especially Hannah."

"She manages fine without my sympathy."

"Is that all it was? Sympathy?"

Gabe wouldn't keep pushing if he didn't think it was important. They had crossed an ocean together, built a settlement together, and followed their fathers into the elder council together. Henry looked across the worktable at his closest friend. "I care for her... very much. But I ruined it."

Gabe removed his elbows from the worktable and slowly straightened his spine like a carpenter whose muscles were tired from working all day. "What happened?"

Henry grabbed a rag and found a dusty spot on the letterpress to wipe so he wouldn't have to look another man in the eye while he talked about his failure. "I made her angry."

"Do you love her?"

He nodded. "But not well enough. She deserves better."

"Better than what?"

"This." He raised his left hand in the air with its scarred stubs pointing at the ceiling. "She deserves a whole man who can build her a house and plow the earth and—"

"You're not a farmer. You're a printer. You were learning to be a printer from your father long before the accident. Your choice of profession has nothing to do with missing a couple of fingers."

"But having only half a hand affects me now. I'm working sixteen hours a day to prove my abilities to the elders so the village will support this trade—"

"Because it's necessary to the settlement."

"Because I cannot do all the rest by myself."

Gabe crossed his arms. "You can fish. You can hunt. You can support yourself and a family as well as any man here."

"But I do not have the time right now to support even myself and certainly don't have the time to give Hannah the attention she needs."

"Is that why you refused to print her story?"

He tossed the rag to the worktable. "How did you know?"

Gabe glanced at the open door then lowered his voice. "I knew Olivia sent Hannah to you to ask about printing it a while back. Then, you and Hannah started getting sweet. And now, the two of you aren't speaking to each other, and Hannah told Olivia she has given up on writing. It wasn't hard to figure out."

"Then why did you ask me?" It wasn't really a question, and Gabe didn't answer.

Henry's hand ached, his shoulders ached, and his tired eyes needed rest. He slid a wooden stool out from under the worktable then sat and blew out a weary breath. "The story needed work. It wasn't ready to be printed. We would both regret it if I printed it as it was just to please her. I told her so. She got upset. Grabbed her things to leave and accidentally knocked burning candles onto my finished pages."

Gabe drew his head back. "That was the fire your father told the elders about in the meeting last month? The fire that put you behind on this project?" He motioned toward the drying pages hanging beside them. "No wonder Hannah quit writing and you're miserable."

"I'm not…" It was no use lying to Gabe, or himself. "My father said to focus on my work for now, and he was right. I can't stop what I'm doing and chase after a girl who won't listen to reason."

"Even a girl you love?"

Henry didn't answer.

Gabe tapped his fingers on the worktable. "You know how long I had to pursue Olivia?"

How could he forget? He'd listened to Gabe moon about her through their school years and well after. "That was different. You wanted a wife and family."

"And you don't?"

The question set off a yearning in his soul. How could he answer a question he'd forced out of his own mind for weeks? Years? He rubbed his sore palm. "I used to. When Jonah was pursuing Marian and you were after Olivia, I thought I'd end up with Peggy. But she was too superficial. Then I was interested in Cecelia, but she was impossible to please. Now with Hannah… I want what every man wants, but I won't spend my life pining over something I can't have."

"Hannah isn't like Peggy or Cecelia."

"You think I should pursue Hannah?"

"I think you should give her grace." Gabe tapped a knuckle on the surface of the table. "That's the one thing Hannah deserves that you aren't giving her. That and patience. I've seen her when she brings her writing to Olivia. She's terrified having someone read her story. She probably felt the same way bringing it to you."

"And I crushed her." The weight of his affection for her squeezed his chest. He looked at Gabe. "I was simply being forthright about her story. Women are impossible. How was I to know she couldn't handle the truth?"

Gabe shrugged. "If I knew the answers, it wouldn't have taken me seven years to get Olivia to marry me." He grinned as he stood to leave. "And women aren't impossible. Not the good ones... girls like Hannah. If you love her, sacrifice your pride for her."

It was fine for Gabe to make it sound simple; he was happily married. Henry had been honest with Hannah and it separated them. And he wouldn't lie. He pushed himself off the stool and paced the floor between the press and the worktable. "What am I to do now?"

Gabe slapped on his hat as he walked to the door. "You'll think of something."

CHAPTER TWENTY-FOUR

Hannah squinted from the afternoon sunlight as she stepped out of the schoolhouse. With her chin raised, she strode down the sandy road toward the print shop. It took a month of late nights, but she'd rewritten her story, filling it with both romantic satisfaction and realistic loss. "Thank you, Lord," she whispered toward the sky.

Adeline had found her true love, but she would never see her family or homeland again. Aric was crowned king, but his father drank himself to death before they could be reconciled. Despite their losses, they could face the future because of what they had learned through hardship, because of their faith in God, and because they had each other.

Olivia's favorable opinion still rang in her ears. *The depth of your characters made me feel like I knew them in real life.*

Hannah not only knew them, she'd seen them through their darkest moments. Creating their journeys had helped her on her own.

She closed her satchel's leather flap. Thanks to her father for trading with Mr. Roberts for paper and to Olivia for a final proofreading, Hannah held two handwritten copies of *Between Two Moons*, a story of worlds colliding as two hearts became one. She would wrap one copy for her father's upcoming birthday. The other copy was for Henry—whether he wanted it or not.

On the road ahead, Mr. Owens stopped his buckboard and climbed down to check a wheel. He crouched by the side and stuck his head under the wagon, muttering all the while.

"Good afternoon, Mr. Owens," Hannah said as she bypassed him in the grass.

Mr. Owens's muffled response came from beneath the wagon, but he didn't draw his head out to see who had spoken to him.

Hannah marched on, determined to deliver the manuscript to Henry and leave the print shop before another argument broke out. If he tried to harpoon her verbally, it would be a one-sided argument though, as she would have none of it.

Flecks of quartz glistened in the stone library's stalwart facade as Hannah passed. So much work had already gone into the settlement's library. Mr. Owens and his sons had spent months cutting and fitting the stone. Gabe and his father had built the walls and shelves inside. And Henry had been charged with filling those shelves with books. Since Hannah hoped to one day visit the library and read stories of love and adventure, she should do her best to make amends with the administrator.

She gripped her satchel's strap as she passed the front of the print shop and stood in the doorway. Her nervous feet paused at the threshold. Henry's back faced the door.

He was spinning a handle down a crank on the press. She waited until he finished the process before she stepped inside. "Henry."

He released the handle and spun on his heel. "Hannah." His fingers combed his hair and straightened his collar, but his feet didn't advance toward her. "What can I do for you?" A vulnerable catch in his voice betrayed his attempt at professionalism.

She briefly considered making up some other reason for being there. Perhaps saying she needed paper for the twins. No. She came here with a purpose and wasn't backing down now. She opened her satchel and withdrew his copy of the story. "I brought you this. It's my revised and edited story. Olivia says it's better than any story she has read."

Henry opened his mouth to speak, so she raised a halting hand before he could refuse her offering. "I don't expect you to print it or bind it. I want you to have it in case you might like to read it someday."

As he accepted the twine-bound stack of pages, she rubbed her empty hands together and kept talking, not leaving him a chance to speak. "You were right about the ending. There are no happily ever afters in real love. It's messy and complex because life is messy and complex. Falling in love is more rare than fiction would have us believe, and that kind of love isn't what sustains a relationship. True love isn't a romantic fairy tale. I understand that now."

After weeks of not speaking to him, being in his presence felt like going home and like being a stranger in a foreign land all at once. If she could say what she needed to say and leave quickly, he wouldn't have the chance to reject her again. She closed her satchel and took a step back. "Anyway, I am sorry for setting your pages ablaze. I didn't mean to. You had every right to be angry with me. I came to apologize for my behavior and also to thank you… for everything."

Her voice tightened on a swell of emotion. She should have turned and walked away, but every moment she'd spent with him flashed before her mind. The inspiration that sparked the night he'd danced her across the grass beside the schoolhouse. The surprise of his lips against hers when he'd kissed her on that sunny afternoon at the springs. The feeling of being special when he'd sat by her in church. The comfort of being safe in his arms after he'd saved her from the flood. She could only muster a fraction of her volume as she continued speaking. "You inspired me more than you will ever know, Henry Roberts. And I thank you."

His eyes widened, bringing light to his pale blue irises. "Hannah, I…" He looked down at the manuscript in his hands and pressed his lips together.

She couldn't tell if she'd shocked him or embarrassed him. He had never been wordless before. Maybe he was put off by her candor. Or embarrassed for her humility. He shouldn't be; she'd put away her pride and embraced the life God had given her—talents and responsibilities and obstacles and all.

Her feet scuffled backward to the door and her hand managed a polite wave. "I won't take any more of your time. Good day."

Mr. Owens squeezed around her in the doorway. "Excuse me, young lady." He held up a thin wedge of wood. "Henry, have you got a mallet I can borrow?"

"Of course, Mr. Owens," Henry answered.

Hannah turned to leave, but Henry said her name. She stopped and looked back, hoping for a bent knee and pronouncement of love. "Yes?"

Holding the manuscript in his good hand, he pointed at it with the other. "Thank you."

She gave a short nod and left with the image of Henry holding her pages. She'd said what she came to say, and he hadn't argued. It gave her hope they could be civil toward one another, maybe even be friends again someday. But did he care enough to read her story?

.

CHAPTER TWENTY-FIVE

As soon as Henry helped to fix Mr. Owens's wagon wheel, he sat at the worktable in his quiet print shop and untied the twine on Hannah's manuscript. Written in ink, the measured scrolls of her delicate handwriting conveyed strength and intelligence.

Henry remembered when she'd first asked him to print the story. He'd found her illogical and doubted she could finish writing it, though deep down he'd hoped she would so they could spend more time together. Then, when she'd finished it, he'd found it incompetent and had ruined their relationship before it had the strength to withstand its first storm.

He couldn't change the past, and wasn't sure how he would if he could, but if the closest he would get to her was to read her writing, he would absorb every word.

The afternoon slipped into evening as he turned the pages, unable to peel himself from the adventurous world Hannah created. He was immersed in life as a prince who was fighting to find his way in the world. With each chapter he wanted the maiden to want him more, but what she needed most was to complete her own journey victoriously.

Hannah Vestal continued to be full of surprises, and each one made Henry love her more.

As the sun set, Henry's stomach grumbled, wanting dinner. Not even hunger could stop him from reading—nay, living—the adventure alongside Prince Aric as he fought insurmountable battles, both on the field and in his heart. There was something familiar about the prince and it drew Henry deep into the story. Needing more light, he reached for the oil lantern and turned the dial, increasing its flame.

Hannah had been right in that she empowered her story with emotion, but he hadn't expected it to affect him, to stir him, to give him the desires of the characters. But it did.

While crickets and toads filled the warm air outside the print shop with their nighttime song, Henry turned to the last page in Hannah's story. Alas, the prince had found Adeline. She was not helpless in the prison where she'd been in the original ending, but was tending to wounded soldiers in a makeshift hospital tent she'd erected outside the castle gates. She didn't fling herself into the prince's arm this time. Instead, she asked him to help her lift a patient from a gurney. Together, Aric and Adeline faced the future with hope.

After Henry read the final sentence, he straightened the pages, squaring the corners with the worktable's edge. He looked at his scarred hand and rubbed its sore palm. His missing fingers were no excuse for his inability to open his heart to Hannah. Nor was his desire for perfection. No matter how honest he thought he'd been, his claim of being incapable of loving well was a lie. And finding faults in others was a flimsy front.

Hannah's excellent story should be printed, if not only for her and her father, for the settlement, for the students, and for the generations to come.

He thumbed through the manuscript, counting the pages then made calculations for printing and binding four copies. Why four, he didn't know. She might not want that many copies, but he would give her the option.

He checked the calendar that hung on the wall beside the window. Two weeks until Christopher Vestal's birthday, which was when Hannah had wanted the bound book. Three weeks until the settlement's eighth anniversary celebration, which was when the New Testament project was due.

He noted the days on his paper and calculated the pages. It would not be easy to finish both in time; in fact, his calculations proved it impossible. But Gabe had been right: he needed to put off his pride and give himself up for Hannah. He loved her and had to try to meet her needs, even if it meant not finishing the elders' assignment and ruining his chance at having a village-supported trade.

As he glanced at the calendar once more, movement outside the window caught his eye. The village elders and their firstborn sons were walking from their homes toward the chapel for the weekly meeting. He checked his pocket watch. It was time for him to join them.

His father was standing on the road, speaking with Mr. Foster. Christopher Vestal was walking with Mr. McIntosh. David Vestal was trailing behind them, looking sullen. When he spotted David alone, he rummaged through a stack of papers on a shelf by the letterpress and found the anonymous notes of warning he'd received earlier in the summer.

Once he and Hannah had stopped speaking, the notes had stopped showing up. Still, he'd never confronted David, and if he was going to try to win Hannah back, he didn't want to worry about her petulant brother causing them grief.

A quick turn of the lantern's dial put out the flame. He pulled the print shop door closed behind him. With a careful turn of the doorknob, he left its mark so he would know if anyone entered while he was away, though he hoped a conversation with David Vestal would end such intrusions.

"David," he called out as he crossed the street.

The young man looked up. So did Mr. Vestal and Mr. McIntosh, but both of the older men looked away as they continued their conversation and walked toward the chapel.

David didn't advance to meet Henry in the road, as any considerate man might do, but at least he stopped where he was. He furrowed his freckled brow. "What do you want?"

Henry stopped within arm's reach of Hannah's brother. He kept his voice quiet enough not to be heard by the other men, but forceful enough to let David know he was serious. "I need to speak with you about Hannah."

"Haven't you caused enough trouble?"

He had to ignore the young man's insults if he was going to be heard. "I care about your sister very much."

"Did you care about Cecelia Foster too?"

How did everyone in the settlement know about his failures? He drew a long breath. "I cared about her, yes.

Still do, but not in the way I care about Hannah. Your sister is very special to me."

"Then why did you hurt her?"

"I never meant to, and I will make it right."

"So?"

"So, you should know I have your father's blessing to court her."

"Well, you don't have mine."

He almost chuckled at the young man's ignorance. "I don't need yours."

David propped his fists on his hips and leveled his gaze but said nothing.

Henry opened the folded notes. "I know you don't think much of me, and I don't need you to. But trying to threaten me with these notes won't make me ignore the fact that I love Hannah. And it will only upset her if she finds out you've been doing this."

David scowled at the notes as he read them. "I didn't write that. I don't like you, but I'm not a coward. I don't write notes. I agree with whoever wrote them though. You should stay away from her. You aren't any good for my sister. I've told her so."

Henry stared down at the slips of paper and slowly folded them. If David hadn't written them, who had?

He stuffed the notes into his shirt pocket along with his calculations to print her story. "I will make things right with Hannah. If she will have me, I'll spend my life devoted to her happiness. I will love her until the day I die."

David's brow relaxed. "She deserves that. But she's busy raising the girls. She promised our mother she would take care of them, and you'd be a selfish fool to keep her from it."

The other men were filing into the chapel. Henry needed to join them, but not as much as he needed to make his point. "I will not lead Hannah to do anything that might hurt her family—and that includes you. I know you depend on her, but do you expect her to live with you forever?"

David pushed a hand through his hair and looked at the sky. Finally, he returned his gaze to Henry and shook his head. "No. She deserves to have her own family, but only with a man who is good enough for her." He took a step toward the chapel and pointed at Henry as he passed. "You have a long way to go to prove you're that man."

CHAPTER TWENTY-SIX

B efore daybreak, the glow of morning light turned Hannah's bedroom curtains from a neutral tan to a warm rose. The house was quiet. She tossed off the bedclothes and opened the bottom drawer of her dresser. There beneath her woolen shawl was the handwritten copy of her story she'd wrapped in a scrap of muslin fabric and tied with ribbon.

After a quick change into her day dress, she left the bedroom and carefully closed the door, hoping Doris wouldn't awaken. She stood still for a moment and listened for any noise in the house. No one seemed to be stirring.

If her siblings knew she was giving her father a story for his birthday, they would surely ruin the moment. David would mock the gift. Wade would get angry but not say if it was at her having their father's approval or at David's jesting. Doris would fill the air with her romantic suggestions without knowing the storyline. The twins would probably ask for paper so they could quickly scribble out a story and give it to him too.

Hannah had worked too hard on granting her father's request to have her efforts minimized by sibling rivalry. She hid the wrapped manuscript under a tea towel and set it in front of her father's place at the kitchen table. Wanting today to appear like any other morning, she began her kitchen work by lighting the woodchips that waited in the stove's firebox.

A few minutes after sunrise, Christopher's bedroom door creaked. He padded into the kitchen, hoisting his suspender straps over his shoulders. "Good morning, Hannah."

"Happy birthday, Father." She lifted the tea towel and pulled her father's chair out, inviting him to sit. "I wanted to give you your present now. Hopefully, it will start your birthday off right."

"How kind!" He grinned boyishly and hurried to the chair, sitting slowly with a stiffness that attested to his age. He rubbed his hands together rapidly and glanced at her over his moving fingertips. As he opened the cloth and revealed the manuscript, his eyes widened. "Hannah, is this your—"

"My story. Yes."

He picked it up, his mouth agape. "You finished it."

"For you. Happy birthday."

"For me?"

"And Mother." Emotion broke her voice. "I wanted to honor her memory by finishing it and honor your strength and compassion by giving it to you on your fiftieth birthday."

The tip of his nose and his eyelids reddened. "Your mother was so proud of you. She would be delighted to see the woman you have become."

That commendation meant more to her than any other. Her father sniffed and blinked rapidly as he trailed a finger over the title page. Finally, he cleared his throat. "*Between Two Moons*. How did you come up with that title?"

A smile tugged at her lips. "During an important scene, the main character, Adeline, is sitting beside a pond at night, alone and confused. She looks across the water to see someone who cares for her coming toward her. The moon is shining brightly in the sky above him, and it's also reflected in the water in front of him. For a moment it looks to her as though he is standing between two moons."

Christopher drew his head back slightly. "You have put a lot of thought into this story."

She shrugged one shoulder. "Only about eight years."

"God makes all things beautiful in His time." He covered her hand with his. "Does your story have a happy ending?"

"You must read it to find out."

He squinted, still grinning. "Not even a hint?"

"No. You'll be the first person to read it straight through without having read a previous version, without remembering all my wrong turns."

He leaned back in his seat, gazing proudly at the manuscript. "This is wonderful. I look forward to reading it. And," he held up a finger, "I know how important your privacy is, so I will keep this gift to myself."

"Thank you."

"I'll go tuck it under my mattress now." He re-wrapped it in the cloth but handed her the ribbon. "Thank you, Hannah. I know how hard you worked. And it wasn't easy with a house full of mouths to feed, but you succeeded. You have seen how others can affect your work. I hope you will see how your work might affect others. And I still think you should use your talents to bless this community, not just me."

She ran the silky ribbon between her fingertips. "I'm thinking so too. I'd like to write stories for the library and the school. It might take me a while with a household to tend to but—"

"It's time we divided your chores between your sisters."

She shook her head. "I promised Mother I'd take care of everything."

"Which I believe included teaching the girls how to manage a household." He lifted her chin with a knuckle. "Your mother didn't mean for you to be stuck here forever. She would want you to move forward in life. It's time."

Her heart thumped in her chest, excited over words she never thought she would hear. "Time for me to move forward?"

"You have done a beautiful job with the girls and the house and me." Christopher relaxed his wise brow. "It's time to see what else God has for you in life."

Footsteps moved about in the upstairs bedroom. Christopher glanced at the ceiling and tucked the manuscript under his arm. "Let the girls do more of the housework and you spend that time writing. If you find a new life presenting itself, you are free to pursue it."

She thought of Henry and his unreadable expression when she'd given him the completed manuscript. It didn't appear they would have a future together, but maybe someday they could work together to produce books for the settlement. Or she could write the stories and give them to Olivia to use in school. Maybe a new life was presenting itself.

CHAPTER TWENTY-SEVEN

Henry lifted one of the four printed and bound books on his worktable. The binding stitches were perfect, the pages precisely cut, and the tanned leather exterior beautifully embossed with gold leaf. He traced a finger over the title. *Between Two Moons.*

The urge to flip through the pages tempted him to open the unread books, but he wanted Hannah to be the first to have that honor. After carefully wrapping each volume in a sheet of paper, he slid them one by one into his satchel then checked his pocket watch. Eight o'clock in the morning seemed too early to visit her house, but he wanted to deliver the books soon so she could give one to her father for his birthday. He slung the satchel over his shoulder, keeping his arm across it to guard its precious contents.

The road north was empty, save for a family of songbirds pecking at a pile of seed that must have spilled from a wagon bed. Warm sunrays danced between the trees as Henry shuffled down the road, whistling. The birds launched into flight as he passed their buffet, but he didn't miss a note of his happy tune.

It had been too long since he'd engaged in such a jovial activity as whistling, but everything about this morning, his future, and life in the Land stirred music in his heart. The tunes themselves came from something much deeper than the fine morning: they flowed out of an overwhelming sense of freedom. He was free to do the work he enjoyed and do it on his terms. He was free to build his home when and where he wanted or sleep in the corner of his print shop if he chose. And, most importantly, he was free to love the woman who had captured his heart.

As he neared his family's home, his mother was sweeping the front porch. When she saw him walking down the road, she leaned her broom against the railing and dashed into the house. A moment later she returned to the porch with Ellenore and Hazel. As Henry passed the house, his mother and sisters smiled and waved, giggling with the knowledge of where he was going and why.

"Good luck!" Ellenore called from the porch. She blew a kiss.

He flashed them the confident grin they were hoping for then returned his focus to the road ahead. His self-assurance came not from the hope that Hannah would accept his apology but from his belief that even if she didn't, he was doing the right thing.

Since the Vestals' home was the farthest from the center of the settlement, the sandy road dwindled to a thin path as it veered away from the meadow and toward their house. The perfect rows of stately fruit trees set Mr. Vestal's orchard apart from every other farm in Good Springs.

Movement between two of the rows caught Henry's eye as he passed. At first, he thought it was David mowing the grass around the trees. When Henry got a better view, he realized it was Wade.

The young man stilled his scythe, and a disapproving expression puckered his face. He dropped the tool and marched toward Henry. "What are you doing here?"

Henry halted on the path. He thought of the anonymous notes he'd received that warned him to leave Hannah alone. Shifting his satchel, he withdrew the folded scraps of paper from a side pocket. "I believe these messages were from you."

Wade stopped his hasty approach and leaned his palm against the trunk of the last tree in the orchard's row. His cheeks flushed and he narrowed his eyes. "But you ignored them and you hurt her, didn't you?"

Henry stuffed the notes into his shirt pocket. "You're right, and for that I have come to apologize." When Wade's expression lightened, Henry held up a finger. "To her. Not to you." The scowl returned, so Henry continued. "You cannot expect a man to obey an anonymous note that is tossed into his workplace tied to a rock, can you?"

Wade's face relaxed so that he no longer looked like he'd licked pinesap. He crossed his arms over his chest. The young man wanted to be seen as a hulking man, but the gesture did nothing to increase his stature.

Henry stepped forward. "Hannah and I have had our differences, but I'm here to do my best to make it right. Do you find something ignoble in that?"

Wade crinkled his brow. "Are you going to tell her you're sorry?"

He almost grinned. "Yes, and I brought something that I hope will rectify the situation."

"Will it make her happy?"

Henry patted his satchel. "I believe it will make her very happy indeed."

The young man lowered his arms, his shoulders slumping slightly. "I want her to be happy."

"Me too. I care about Hannah very much. I can't promise that we will never argue again—in fact, that's half the fun—but I will strive to always treat her kindly." Henry stepped closer, seeking to build camaraderie with the young man who, as a second son, must have felt left out among the village men. "If she is able to forgive me, might you be able to as well?"

Wade shrugged one shoulder. "I suppose, but you better not hurt her again."

"And since you have shown the courage to warn me in person, man to man, I shall take your warning to heart." Henry straightened his hat as if on his way to official business. "Now if you will be so kind as to let me pass, sir, I must pour my heart out at the feet of the woman I love."

Wade laughed once. "Are you going to say that to her?"

"Probably not." He grinned at Wade. "Unless you believe it will help my chances of winning her back."

"No, I want to be there to see it if you do."

He patted Wade's shoulder as he passed. "I'm sure you will have ample opportunity to laugh at my blunders in the future."

As Henry cut across the yard, one of the Vestals' yellow dogs ran beneath the clothesline with four puppies following it. The last puppy turned toward a tablecloth that wiggled in the wind. The puppy caught the edge of the cloth in its teeth and tugged playfully.

"No, no, no!" Hannah yelled at the puppy as she stormed out of the mudroom to the clothesline.

The puppy continued having its fun with the cloth until Hannah scooped it from the ground and opened its furry jaw. As soon as she'd freed her laundry from the puppy's mouth, she hugged the dog to her chest. "My laundry is not a toy for you, understand?"

The puppy licked Hannah's chin and she smiled.

Henry was only a stone's throw behind her when she looked back. Her gaze traced the length of him, from the top of his felt hat down to his polished boots and back up, finally settling on his face. She cradled the puppy with one arm and petted its head with the other hand.

He gave her the chance to speak first. When she said nothing, he removed his hat and walked toward her. "My apologies for coming uninvited and so early in the day. I have something for you. A delivery from the print shop."

Hannah lowered the puppy to the ground and watched as it ran after its mother. Then she met his gaze. "Something for me?"

"Yes," he answered, opening his satchel. He paused to scan the property. Wade was watching them from the orchard. Doris and the twins were in the vegetable patch, though they were looking in the opposite direction. There was movement in the barn, but with the laundry flapping back and forth in his line of sight, he couldn't tell if it was Christopher or David. "May we step inside?"

She raised her regal chin, looking at the back door of the house and spoke with an edge in her voice. "Very well. But I have work to do."

"I won't be long, I promise." He followed her through the door, which was propped open with a wedge of wood, and up the mudroom steps into the kitchen. The buttery scent of johnnycakes clung to the air, making his stomach grumble.

She stopped in front of the stove and spoke over her shoulder. "I can put the kettle on, if you want a cup of tea. And there are biscuits," she said, motioning to a covered breadbasket on the table. "I have apple jam too, if you like."

"No, thank you." Though he had worked through the night and his body begged for sustenance, he had come to fulfill the purpose of his work not feed his belly. He stepped past her to the table and set down his satchel. "Thank you for the honor of reading your story."

"You read it?" She breathed the question with hesitation.

"Olivia was right. It's one of the best stories I have ever read. Absolutely inspired."

She tucked a stray wisp of hair behind her ear and turned to face him. "Do you really think so?"

His hands yearned to reach for her. "I wouldn't say so if I didn't mean it."

She nodded rigidly. "No. I know. You've been quite honest in your assessments." A sweet smile broke through, banishing the sadness from her eyes. "*Inspired*, you say?"

"Exquisitely." He almost smiled as he pulled the wrapped books from his satchel. It was too soon to be satisfied. He stacked the first three of the books on the table and then held out the fourth to her. "Your story deserved to be printed. I worked night and day until it was done."

Her lips parted in surprise as she accepted the book. Before she unwrapped the paper, she looked up at him with a slight furrow between her delicately arched brows. "Had you already finished your assignment from the elders?"

"No." He was too far behind now to finish. "This was more important."

"More important than making your profession a village-supported trade?"

"You are more important." He lifted his chin at the book. "Open it."

As she unwrapped the book, paper crackled then floated to the table. She held the book with both hands, her joy-filled face like a mother examining her newborn. She touched the embossed letters then lifted the cover. *"Between Two Moons by Hannah Vestal. Printed in Good Springs in the Year of Our Lord 1869.* It's gorgeous. Henry, I..." Her golden brown eyes left the book long enough to glance at him. "I don't know what to say."

"You deserve it."

"No, I don't."

"You worked hard and used the talents God gave you to write a story the whole settlement needs to read." He waited for her to recoil, but she didn't. He tapped the other three copies stacked on the table. "One copy is for your father. I'd hoped to deliver it early so you could give it to him for his birthday. The other two copies are yours to do with as you wish, but I'm hoping one copy will be donated to the library."

"I'll have to think about it." She closed the book's cover and hugged it to her chest as lovingly as she had cuddled the puppy a moment ago.

"Yes, of course. And talk it over with Olivia and your father since they know your feelings on the matter and would give you wise counsel."

She smiled. "I already know what they would say."

"As do I." He stepped forward, closing the distance between them. "Take your time and think it over. I never want to rush you."

"You have been so kind."

"No, I haven't. I have been honest with you but not kind. I will never lower my standards, but I'm determined to give the same grace that I need every day. You came to me and asked for my forgiveness when I was the one who should have apologized. I've made so many excuses for myself and refused to excuse others. No more."

She laid the book on the table. "I know I don't make sense sometimes, and—"

"But you do. After reading your story, I feel like I finally understand you. Not fully but enough. You make sense to me." His heart drove him to plead for hers. He took her fingers in his good hand. "Hannah, I know you are bound by promise to help raise your sisters, and that's part of what I admire about you. So, I will wait for you. In the meantime, would you let me court you?"

Gazing into his eyes, she took his left hand in hers, touching the scars as if they were perfect skin. "I'd like that very much."

He drew her hands to his lips and kissed them. "Thank you." He almost said that she'd made him the happiest man in the village, and indeed every fiber of his being pulsed with joy. However, he would wait to tell her on the day he proposed marriage. For now, he would try to make her the happiest woman.

The warmth of her hand radiated through his scars. He looked down at his aching hand. "Does it bother you?"

"No." She replied quickly then gazed up at him. "Does it bother you?"

"Sometimes. But it won't keep me from anything." He released her hands and reached into his satchel. "I have one more thing for you. I meant to give it to you months back, but the timing didn't feel right." He withdrew the sketch of her mother. "I drew this long ago. I want you to have it."

She covered her mouth with four thin fingertips. "Henry!" she gasped.

"I tried to capture your mother's likeness as she was when she babysat my brother and me as children."

"It's perfect." She dabbed the corner of her eyes. "Sometimes when I try too hard to remember what she looked like, I can't picture her at all. But this," she said, holding the sketch as if it were a treasure map, "is more than I've ever wanted."

"I'm glad you like it."

"I'll ask my father to build a frame." She stepped toward the parlor. "And we will hang it on the wall. I know the perfect place."

He followed her into the next room while she held the sketch up to the wall. Seeing her joyful was more satisfying than any accomplishment, any argument won, any perfection. He leaned against the corner and watched her, filled with contentment.

CHAPTER TWENTY-EIGHT

Hannah tightened her shawl around her shoulders as she mingled with the villagers at the settlement's eighth anniversary celebration. The autumn equinox's arrival had brought a chill to the air. Soon the deciduous leaves would change colors, painting the village in splashes of red and gold.

Autumn was her favorite time of the year and it always began with the village's anniversary festivities. She'd never been more pleased to celebrate coming to the Land than she was this year. For it was this special place that had opened her imagination, lured her to write, and inspired her with its beauty. In her arms she held two copies of her book, proof of what the right inspiration could help to accomplish.

Several booths had been set up on the dry grass in front of the chapel. An array of fresh pies and cookies and pastries covered one table. The glassblower stood behind another table offering each child a miniature figurine as a commemorative token. Mrs. Foster sat at one end of a table, showing children how to re-bristle a bone toothbrush, while Mrs. Colburn stood behind the other end, demonstrating how to make salt-based dentifrice. Minnie and Ida intently watched the ladies. Hopefully, the girls would come home with a keen interest in dental health.

Hannah rubbed her fingertips along the spines of the books she held as she stood on her tiptoes to scan the crowd for Olivia. Gabe spoke with a group on the other side of the chapel steps. As Hannah wove through the crowd, she spotted Olivia beside him and waved.

Olivia rushed to meet her with eyes growing wide as they landed on the books Hannah held. "Is this it? May I see it?"

Hannah's hope of surprising Olivia deflated. "How did you…?" She looked past Olivia at Gabe. "Henry told your husband, didn't he?" She handed Olivia one book.

As soon as Olivia took it, she hugged Hannah then beamed as she opened the front cover. "It's beautiful! *Between Two Moons by Hannah Vestal.* Can you believe your name is on a book—an actual book? If it were mine, I'd stare at it all the time, getting nothing else done."

"I've read it twice from cover to cover since Henry brought it to me last week. He printed four copies—one for me, one for my father, and two that I get to choose what to do with. I want you to have this copy."

Olivia looked up from the book. Astonishment filled her voice. "You want me to have it?"

"Yes. I couldn't have accomplished this—wouldn't have—without you. From that dark night seven years ago when you sat with me in my parents' kitchen and read my first pitiful pages—"

"They weren't pitiful—"

"They weren't printable."

"Now you sound like Henry."

Hannah laughed. "I've learned a lot from him too." She lowered her voice. "We are courting now."

Olivia flashed a knowing grin. "So I heard."

"From Gabe?"

"Of course."

It was a good thing she considered Olivia a dear friend, seeing as how there weren't many secrets between Henry and Gabe. It was even better that she knew whatever Olivia learned from her husband would be kept between them.

Olivia pressed the book to her chest. "Thank you. I will cherish it always."

"Thank you for all of your help and guidance and editing. You put almost as much work into this story as I did."

Olivia chuckled. "Oh, I wouldn't go that far."

"It meant a great deal to me. I depended on you in a lot of ways after my mother died, but you never minded."

"Not only did I not mind, I enjoyed our times together. I hope you write more stories and keep bringing your pages to me."

She nodded, grateful to have Olivia's continued support. "I will."

Olivia tilted her head and looked at the other copy, which Hannah was still holding. "What will you do with the fourth book?"

Hannah glanced across the road at the stone building next to the print shop. The library's arched door stood open. "Well, since you enjoyed the story so much and Henry called it *absolutely inspired* and Father finished it last night with tears in his eyes... I think I should donate this copy to the village library."

"That's wonderful news!" Olivia lightly squeezed her arm. "I know it will bless many readers over the years."

"That's the only reason I'm making my story public." She motioned toward the crowd. "For them. For my village."

Olivia nodded. "I would like to teach from the story for the upper grades next year. And maybe someday you could help to create new school readers for the lower grades."

"Maybe." Hannah turned toward the library. "But I have to start with this small step first."

"You can do it," Olivia encouraged.

Hannah nodded and walked away from the crowded lawn to cross the road. Dr. and Mrs. Ashton stepped out of the library as she approached. Dr. Ashton tipped his hat to her as he passed. "What a skilled young man Henry is," he was saying to his wife.

Henry stood inside the library with his back to the door, whistling. His fingers turned the page of a book on a lectern in the center of the room. Hannah's heels clicked on the stone floor as she entered.

Henry turned around. He smiled and opened his arms. "Hannah," he breathed as he kissed the top of her head.

She pulled back, wishing she wasn't holding a book. She imagined jumping into his arms and kissing him wildly. Her cheeks instantly warmed.

Henry cocked his head. "What is that look?"

"Nothing." She giggled once then composed herself and pointed at the lectern. "What's this?"

He stepped back and gestured toward the book. "This is an error-free copy of the New Testament, printed by yours truly."

She stepped forward and studied the open book. Its regal lettering proclaimed the Good News. "You finished it. You met the elders' challenge. So is it official then? Will the press be supported by the village?"

Henry rubbed the palm of his scarred hand with the thumb of the other. "I've been granted the living, but I've refused it."

"What? Why?"

"Because I don't need to be taken care of. I can take care of myself. I can print enough books to trade with everyone in the village to get the things I need. I don't want to be a special case. Yes, I believe we should honor the reverend and schoolteachers and physicians with our abundance, to ensure that they can always continue their work. We should all do our part for the village. I will print the books we need because that is the work I've been called to do. Gabe and his father have offered to help me build living rooms onto the shop, and Mr. Foster will help me plant a vegetable patch next spring."

Hannah's heart filled with pride in Henry and with happy anticipation for the possibilities in their future. She glanced at all the empty shelves in the library. "So you are going to spend your life filling these shelves with books?"

He stepped to the shelves and his excited expression grew. "And not just any books. I realized how easily our skills and crafts and processes could be lost from one generation to the next. We can't allow that. So, I want to start a new tradition. At the next elders' meeting, I will propose a system of documenting everyone's life knowledge."

"I think the elders will approve."

"I hope so." He walked back to where she stood and looked at the book in her hands. "You didn't come only to see me, did you?"

She smiled at him and shook her head. "In honor of this festive occasion and in honor of the printer who inspired me more than he will ever know, I'd like to make a donation to this library."

Henry's admiring gaze shifted from her eyes to the book she held out and back to her eyes. "Are you certain you want your story to be read by anyone and everyone?"

"Yes. And I plan to write many more stories, if the village printer is willing to work with me... when the stories are ready to be printed, of course."

"I am more than willing." He accepted the book then leaned down and kissed her.

She absorbed his warmth and closed her eyes, blissfully aware of the new life unfolding before her. There was one person she wished she could tell, and she would visit the grave later, much later. For now, she would let Henry kiss her and love her and postulate his logical arguments and urge her to greater ambitions while she dreamed up her next story.

EPILOGUE

The village of Good Springs
Late summer, 2025

On a quiet evening, Lydia Colburn sat on the parlor rug, reading aloud to her great aunt, Isabella. While the elderly blind woman knitted, Lydia turned the final page of her favorite novel.

"There is much to be done for these people, for this kingdom, and I will not sit idly in a castle, fussing over jewels and ball gowns,' Adeline said. She draped a threadbare blanket over a wounded solider then rounded the patient cot. Her kind gaze met Prince Aric's. 'But if you are most willing to bring peace to your kingdom,' she touched his lapel, 'then yes, my love, I will marry you.'

Adeline's heart brimmed with hope—not in the man before her, nor for the work around her, but in the God who had set eternity in their hearts and would one day make all things beautiful."

Lydia closed *Between Two Moons* and sighed. "I adore Adeline. Don't you?"

Aunt Isabella's knitting needles clicked rhythmically, her old voice gravelly. "I do. As did your mother."

"She did?"

"That's why she named your eldest sister after the character."

"I never realized that." Lydia considered the story for a moment, its feel and breadth still fresh in her mind. "Do you think when the author wrote it, she knew over a century later people would still get lost in her story?"

Isabella's lips twitched before she spoke, her unseeing gaze roamed the room. "I don't suppose most people know how their work will be received, or if it will be remembered at all."

Lydia touched the embossed letters on the book's cover. "This is the only one of the author's books that says *Hannah Vestal*. All the rest have her married name, Hannah Roberts." She thought of her late mother's given name. "Was Mother named after the author?"

"That I could not say. There have been many women named Hannah in the generations since the eighteen sixties. I'm sure some of them were named after the author. And I suspect there will be a great number of girls named after you, Dr. Lydia Colburn, the first female physician in the Land."

"I'm not a doctor yet. The elders haven't awarded me the title."

Isabella smiled. "Soon enough, child. Soon enough."

Men's voices rumbled in the kitchen, commanding Lydia's attention. Her father, Reverend John Colburn, spoke to some frantic person at the kitchen door. As Lydia stood from the floor, John stepped into the parlor. "Lydia, Mr. McIntosh needs you. His son fell from the roof of their barn and has broken his leg. He is bleeding profusely."

"Where is the boy?"

"Still at home."

Lydia set the book on the doily-covered table beside Isabella and gave her a quick kiss on the cheek. "Good night, Aunt Isabella."

"Be careful, child."

"I will be," she assured her great aunt then dashed out of the room. Two lanterns burned brightly on the kitchen table. She held up a finger as she passed Mr. McIntosh by the door. "I'll just grab my bag from the medical cottage and be on my way."

Mr. McIntosh followed her, wringing his hat in his hands. "You'll find my boy in the back bedroom. Rebecca was making him gray leaf tea when I left. He's bleeding very badly. Please, hurry."

Lydia dashed out the back door of her family's home to her cottage and grabbed her medical bag, which she always kept right inside the office door. "Father will saddle my horse for you," she said to Mr. McIntosh, who was standing beside his chestnut mare between the house and cottage. "I'll take your horse." After buckling her medical bag to Mr. McIntosh's saddle, she jumped onto the mare's back. "Don't worry, Mr. McIntosh. I will do everything in my power to save your son."

If this is your first visit to the Land, continue reading for a preview of *The Land Uncharted*...

CHAPTER ONE

Lydia Colburn refused to allow a child to bleed to death. Pulling a sprig of gray tree leaves out of her wind-whipped hair, she rushed inside the farmhouse and found the injured boy sprawled across the bed exactly as Mr. McIntosh had said she would. She dropped her medical bag on the floor beside Mrs. McIntosh, who was holding a blood-soaked rag against young Matthew's lower leg.

The globe of an oil lamp provided the only light in the dim bedroom. Matthew's breath came in rapid spurts. Lydia touched his clammy skin. "He's still losing blood. Get the pillows out from under his head." She slid her hands beneath his fractured limb and gently lifted it away from the mattress. "Put them here under his leg."

Mrs. McIntosh's thin hands shook as she moved the pillows. "I gave him tea from the gray leaf tree as soon as his father brought him in the house." Her voice cracked. "I know he doesn't feel the pain now, but it hurts me just to look at all this blood."

"You did the right thing." Lydia opened her medical bag and selected several instruments. She peeled back the bloody rag, revealing the fractured bone. Its crisp, white edges protruded through his torn skin. "You're going to be all right, Matthew. Do you feel any pain?"

"No, but it feels weird." His chin quivered as he stared at his mother with swollen eyes. "Am I going to die?"

Mrs. McIntosh drew her lips into her mouth and stroked his head. "You're going to be fine. Miss Colburn will fix it."

When Lydia touched the boy's leg, he recoiled and screamed. It was not from pain but from terror. With his fractured leg tucked close to his body, he buried his face into the pleats of his mother's dress.

Lydia gave Mrs. McIntosh a chance to muster her courage and make her son cooperate, but instead she coddled him. Though Lydia appreciated a nurturing mother, this was no time to help a child hide his wound. "Your mother is right. You're going to be just fine." She reached for his leg again. "You don't have to look at me, but you must leave your leg on the pillow. Matthew? Let me straighten your leg."

Mrs. McIntosh glared at the bloody wound and began to weep. "Oh, Matt, I'm so sorry. My baby!"

"Mrs. McIntosh?" Lydia raised her voice over the woman's sobs. "Rebecca! I know this is hard, but please have courage for Matthew's sake. I need you to help me. Can you do that?"

Mrs. McIntosh sniffled and squared her shoulders. "Yes. I'm sorry, Lydia."

"I need more light. Do you have another lamp in the house?"

"Yes, of course." Mrs. McIntosh wiped her nose on her sleeve and scurried out of the room.

Relieved that Mrs. McIntosh was gone, Lydia caught the boy's eye. She touched his foot with both hands. "Matthew, you must lie still while I work on your leg.

You won't feel any pain since you were a good boy and drank the gray leaf tea your mother made, but now you have to be brave for me and hold still. All right?" She was prepared to hold him down but loathed the thought.

Matthew allowed her to move his broken leg back onto the pillow. She worked quickly and methodically until the bleeding was under control. She cleaned his flesh with gray leaf oil then looked into the open wound and aligned the bone.

Mrs. McIntosh's footsteps echoed in the hallway, but Lydia was not ready for the anxious mother's return. "Please, bring cold water and a few clean rags first. I need them more than I need the extra light." The footsteps receded.

She continued to work. Matthew's eyes were clenched shut. Her heart ached for the pallid and broken boy. "I heard you had a birthday recently, Matthew. How old are you now? Fifteen? Sixteen?"

He opened his eyes but stared at the ceiling. "I'm seven," he slurred through missing teeth. His respiration had settled; the gray leaf's healing power was beginning to take effect.

"Ah, I see you've lost another baby tooth." She cut a piece of silk thread for suture and kept the needle out of his sight while she threaded it. "Soon you will have handsome new adult teeth."

He closed his eyes again and lay still.

Mrs. McIntosh walked back into the room with a pitcher of water in her hands and a wad of kitchen towels tucked under her elbow. She set the water jug on the floor beside Lydia's feet and bundled the rags on the bed. "Is that enough?"

"Yes, thank you."

"I'll be right back with the lamp." Mrs. McIntosh vanished from the room again.

Lydia covered the stitches with a thick layer of gray leaf salve. As she wrapped his leg loosely with clean muslin, the front door slammed and a man's worried voice drifted down the hallway.

Mrs. McIntosh spoke to her husband in a hushed tone and then walked into the bedroom holding a lamp. She sighed. "Oh, thank heavens you're done." She lit the lamp and placed it on a doily-covered table by the bed. As she sat on the edge of the mattress beside Matthew, she whispered, "He's asleep."

Lydia slathered her hands with the disinfecting gray leaf oil and wiped them on a clean rag. As she gathered her medical instruments, Mr. McIntosh stepped in from the bedroom doorway, holding his wide-brimmed hat in his hands.

He cleared his throat. "Is there anything I can do?"

Lydia replied, "I need a couple thin pieces of wood to splint his leg."

Mr. McIntosh nodded and left the house. While he was gone, Lydia cleaned and packed her instruments. A short time later, he returned with two flat wooden shingles. Lydia used them to splint Matthew's leg and gave Mr. and Mrs. McIntosh instructions for bandaging and cleaning their son's wound.

She handed Mrs. McIntosh a jar of gray leaf salve. "Use this twice a day on the wound. With rest and proper use of the medicine, he should heal completely in a few days."

She followed Mr. and Mrs. McIntosh out to the porch. Stars crowded the clear sky, and crickets' intermittent chirps pierced the cool night air. Lydia's horse snorted as Mr. McIntosh gathered the reins and walked it to her.

"Thank you, Lydia." Mrs. McIntosh fanned her face with both hands.

Mr. McIntosh wiped his brow with a cotton handkerchief. "It seems too dangerous of a job for a woman—taking the forest path alone at night like you did to get here." He slapped his hat back on his head and dabbed at the sweat on his neck. "I'm grateful you got here in time to save my boy, no doubt about it, but the way you rushed down the forest path instead of taking the main road worried me. Granted you beat me back here by twenty minutes, but still it's too dangerous at night to—"

"I haven't seen a night dark enough to keep me from my duty." She stepped around Mr. McIntosh and strapped her medical bag to the saddle.

He nodded. "That'll be the last time Matthew climbs to the roof of the barn."

"Yes. Please see to it." She tucked a loose strand of hair behind her ear.

Mr. McIntosh handed her the reins. "I heard your family will be gathering tomorrow night to celebrate Isabella's seventy-fifth birthday. How about I deliver a lamb roast as your payment?"

"I accept. I'll tell my father to expect you." She mounted her horse. "Aunt Isabella will be glad to have roast lamb at her party."

"A lamb it is. Thank you, Miss Colburn. Oh, and do take the road back to the village. I'd never forgive myself if something happened to you on your way home."

...

The Land Uncharted is available now in paperback, ebook, and audiobook.

Thank you for reading my book. I'm so glad you went on this journey with me. More Uncharted stories await you! Are you ready for the adventure?

I know it's important for you to enjoy these wholesome, inspirational stories in your favorite format, so I've made sure all of my books are available in ebook, paperback, and large print versions.

Below is a quick description of each story so that you can determine which books to order next…

The Uncharted Series
A hidden land settled by peaceful people ~ The first outsider in 160 years

The Land Uncharted (#1)
Lydia's secluded society is at risk when an injured fighter pilot's parachute carries him to her hidden land.

Uncharted Redemption (#2)
When vivacious Mandy is forced to depend on strong, silent Levi, she must learn to accept tender love from the one man who truly knows her.

Uncharted Inheritance (#3)
Bethany and Everett belong together, but when a mysterious man arrives in the Land, everything changes.

Christmas with the Colburns (#4)
When Lydia faces a gloomy holiday in the Colburn house, an unexpected gift brightens her favorite season.

Uncharted Hope (#5)
While Sophia and Nicholas wrestle with love and faith, a stunning discovery outside the Land changes everything.

Uncharted Journey (#6)
When horse trainer Solo moves to Falls Creek, widow Eva gets a second chance at love. Meanwhile, Bailey's quest to reach the Land costs her everything.

Uncharted Destiny (#7)
The Uncharted story continues when Bailey and Revel face an impossible rescue mission in the Land's treacherous mountains.

Uncharted Promises (#8)
When Sybil and Isaac get snowed in, it takes more than warm meals and cozy fireplaces to help them find love at the Inn at Falls Creek.

Uncharted Freedom (#9)
When Naomi takes the housekeeping job at The Inn at Falls Creek to hide from one past, another finds her.

Uncharted Courage (#10)
With the survival of the Land at stake and their hearts on the line, Bailey and Revel must find the courage to love.

Uncharted Christmas (#11)
While Lydia juggles her medical practice and her family obligations this Christmas, she is torn between the home life she craves and the career that defines her.

Uncharted Grace (#12)
Caroline and Jedidiah must overcome their shattered pasts and buried secrets to find love in the village of Good Springs.

The Uncharted Beginnings Series
Embark on an unforgettable 1860s journey with the Founders as they discover the Land.

Aboard Providence (#1)
When Marian and Jonah's ship gets marooned on a mysterious uncharted island, they must build a settlement to survive. Love and adventure await!

Above Rubies (#2)
When schoolteacher Olivia needs the settlement elders' approval, she must hide her dyslexia from everyone, even charming carpenter Gabe.

All Things Beautiful (#3)
Henry is the last person Hannah wants reading her story… and the first person to awaken her heart.

Find out more on my website keelybrookekeith.com or feel free to email me at keely@keelykeith.com where I answer every message personally.

See you in the Land!
Keely

About Keely Brooke Keith

Keely Brooke Keith writes inspirational frontier-style fiction with a slight Sci-Fi twist, including *The Land Uncharted* (Shelf Unbound Notable Romance 2015) and *Aboard Providence* (2017 INSPY Awards Longlist).

Born in St. Joseph, Missouri, Keely grew up in a family that frequently relocated. By graduation, she lived in 8 states and attended 14 schools. When she isn't writing, Keely enjoys playing bass guitar, preparing homeschool lessons, and collecting antique textbooks. Keely, her husband, and their daughter live on a hilltop south of Nashville, Tennessee.

For more information or to connect with Keely, visit her website keelybrookekeith.com.